EASTFORD PUBLIC LIBRARY

3 3300 00009     W9-CXM-314

J
GLE

Gleeson, Libby

I am Susannah

$12.95                    i

| DATE | | |
|---|---|---|
| NOV. 09 1989 | | |
| NOV. 21 1989 | | |
| DEC. 9 1990 | | |
| MAR. 23 1993 | | |
| OCT 14 1995 | | |
| MAR 14 1998 | | |
| | | |
| | | |
| | | |
| | | |

EASTFORD PUBLIC LIBRARY
EASTFORD, CT     06242

© THE BAKER & TAYLOR CO.

018840

J
GLE

# I AM
# SUSANNAH

## Libby Gleeson

Holiday House/New York

10/87 15+7  12.95

EASTFORD PUBLIC LIBRARY
EASTFORD, CT    06242

For Lucy and all the other kids who helped

Copyright © Libby Gleeson 1987
First published in Austrialia by Angus & Robertson Publishers
First American publication 1989 by Holiday House, Inc.
Printed in the United States of America

Library of Congress Cataloging-in-Publication Data

Gleeson, Libby.
I am Susannah/written by Libby Gleeson.
p. cm.
Summary: When her best friend Kim moves, Susie goes solo in an
effort to uncover the truth about the mysterious Blue Lady who has
moved into Kim's old house.
ISBN 0-8234-0742-X
[1. Mystery and detective stories.]   I. Title.
PZ7.G48148 Iam      1989
[Fic]—dc19      88-24568      CIP      AC

ISBN 0-8234-0742-X

# I AM
# SUSANNAH

# Chapter 1

Susie and Kim start kindergarten on the same day. Three years old, fight over a one-wheeled scooter and a hairless doll. Friends. Sleep at each other's houses. Lie on the upstairs balcony and blow peas through a straw at kids going past. Sprawl on the bed in Susie's attic and stare at the church spire and the tall golden tower over the city. Run home down King Street, press noses against glass windows, dig up sixty cents from the bottom of tunic pockets and share a sticky cake, sitting on the low brick fence of the doctor's office. At four o'clock in the sun-drenched cemetery, play chasings over the roots of the Moreton Bay fig tree, lie on the warm headstone of the boy who was lost at sea and talk. Friends.

'We're leaving,' said Kim.

Susie didn't hear her. She lay on her back in the warm sun, her eyes half-closed. There was a hum of insects and of traffic on King Street.

'I said we're leaving.' Kim stood up, leant back against an old palm tree and looked down at Susie's face. 'For Melbourne, just like I said we might last year. Only this time it's real. For good.'

'Melbourne!' Susie sat up. 'But . . .'

'It's all arranged. Dad starts work next week . . . with

my uncle. Mum says we can be packed up by the weekend.'
Kim tucked her thumbs into the belt of her tunic and
dragged it down. She kicked a lump of dirt and it shattered
against the metal railing around a headstone. 'We're
stopping at Aunty Joy's place till we get fixed up.'

*Leaving. Kim leaving.*

Susie stared at Kim as she hooked her arm around the
tree and swung out. Her straight black hair fell below her
shoulders.

*Who will I sit with? Kim. Always Kim.*

'Do you want to go?'

'Dunno.' She spun round, her weight on her heel
leaving a small circle of flattened grass. 'Mum does. And
Dad. They've always reckoned it was better. And my
Nanna lives there.' She dived away, four cartwheels, across
the open space to the three-decker tomb. She leapt up onto
the top level and sat, arm around the broken angel, feet
dangling.

'But we're not there. Me and Michelle and Tanya and
Tracey . . . and . . . and . . . Who will you sit with at
school? You won't know anyone.' Susie jumped up and
stood facing Kim. She shielded her eyes from the late
afternoon sun.

Kim looked away from her. 'I'm not starting till after
Christmas. Then I'll go to the same high school as my
cousin Sharon. She's a year ahead but she knows everyone.'
Her voice dropped. 'I'll . . . be OK.'

She pushed herself off the stone and landed on the grass
on her knees. She beckoned Susie. 'Come here, sshh.' She
put her fingers to her lips. 'Look. There she is again.'

Susie spun around. A woman in a blue skirt
disappeared behind the Chinese elm and around the side
of the church.

'And guess what?' said Kim. 'You'll never believe it.

2

Turns out she owns our house. She's moving in after we go.'

'Her!' Susie stared. 'Is that why you're leaving?'

Kim shrugged. 'Can you believe it? That crazy old creep in my bedroom.'

'How come she owns it? You've always lived there.'

Kim kept her eyes on the place where the woman had disappeared. 'It got sold a few months ago. I hate her.'

Susie said nothing. They waited for the woman to reappear.

'Remember,' Susie giggled, 'remember that time we reckoned she was a witch and we mixed up that stew for her made of slugs and snails and mud and milk?'

'And we were too scared to give it to her 'cause we thought she'd turn us into something. Crazy old bat.' Kim jumped up and Susie followed. 'We should have done it. We should have sat up in our tree near the gate and dropped it all over her.' They ran, leaping over the mounds of earth, the fallen stones, till they collapsed breathless in the long grass. They sat and tugged at stalks and slit them with their fingernails till the pieces grew thinner and thinner and finally broke.

'When I'm gone,' said Kim, 'you want to watch it. If you come in here by yourself, you'll probably go crazy like her.'

'Oh, shut up about her.'

*Crazy Blue Lady, wanders around the cemetery all day. Stares right through you. Drawing, always drawing.*

Susie picked up a stick and started to trace the outline of a face in the dust. She added a tall, pointed witch's hat and a mouth with alternate gaps and long jagged teeth. 'I won't even come here.' Then she kicked the dust over what she had drawn. 'So how many days of school have you got left?'

'Four.'

Susie turned away and leant on the upright stone . . .

IN LOVING MEMORY
OF OUR DEAR DEPARTED SON AND BROTHER;
CHARLES AUGUSTUS RICHARD SEDGEWICK (DICKY)
LOST AT SEA WHILE IN THE SERVICE OF HIS COUNTRY
GONE BUT NOT FORGOTTEN.
1870–1888.

She loosened the stone prow of the boat that jutted out above the inscription. It came away and she put her hand into the space behind it. Their special place. A place to leave messages, presents and surprises on days when they didn't see each other. She caught her finger on a jagged corner of stone and the skin tore. She stuffed it into her mouth and sucked the blood. 'Put a letter in here when you leave and I'll get it after you've gone.'

That was Monday.

On Tuesday Susie sat on the grass behind the weathershed. She watched and listened as Kim spoke.

'. . . Melbourne, and we're going to live with my cousin Sharon for a while. She's got a rat's-tail this long.' She spread her thumb and finger as wide apart as possible.

Tracey and Tanya stopped chewing their apples.

'. . . and she's got this boyfriend called Bradley and I met him in the holidays and we all went skating . . .'

*Hate Bradley. Hate Sharon.*

On Wednesday in art Kim said, 'My cousin Sharon says that their school's got a real artist for a teacher and he lets them do pottery in a kiln, not just stupid stuff like this.'

She waved her hand at the squashed hand-shaped bowls. *Hate Sharon. Hate Melbourne.*

On Thursday Mr Marsden said in language, 'We'll all be sorry to see you go, Kim. We'll all write you letters in class, then you'll get thirty different ones and have to answer them all. Ha. Ha.'
*Hate Marsden. Hate school.*

*Kim, don't go.*

On Friday there was only Susie.

On Friday Susie sat by herself in arithmetic and language. For art, Mrs Chamberlain made her share paint water with Sonya Mitchell.
'Has Kim gone yet?' she asked, leaning across to reach turquoise.
Susie shook her head. 'She's going this afternoon. Before school finishes.'
'You going to go and say goodbye?'
'No.'
Two phone calls and a fleeting visit. Kim out every night saying goodbye to family, her parents' friends.
In P.E. she had to work with Sonya again. 'Do you want to come over to our place this afternoon?' Sonya said. 'My sister's got this new record by Uncanny X-Men. It's great.'
'No, I can't. I have to meet Mum.'
'What about at the weekend?'
'I'll ask.'
'I'll ring you up.'
Susie shrugged.
*Don't bother.*

She walked home by herself along King Street. Straight past the hot bread shop, the cakes and fruit, the bright

5

taffeta dresses on the footpath in front of the secondhand shop. Down Church Street past the doctor's to the open gates of the church and cemetery. She climbed onto the roots of the giant Moreton Bay fig tree and smelt the sweet new-mown grass. The sun touched the side of the church, making it yellow. *I won't even come here.* She ran down the path and turned right at the anchor under the palm trees. She pulled aside the stone prow and felt behind it. Nothing. She scraped all round, felt the tiny grains of weathered stone, the smooth edges from the stonemason's axe. Nothing. *How could she have forgotten?* Susie stood, cold in the sunlight for a long time. Then she turned away and went slowly down the path, out the gate and around to the park bench where she waited for her mother.

'Suse!' Her mother was coming along the path that cut diagonally through the park. She went round the cricket match that David from over the back and his mates were playing and nodded to the man from the paper shop who was walking his dog.

'Did you have a good day, love?'

Susie shrugged. 'O.K.'

'No Kim, eh?'

Susie shook her head. She pressed her lips tightly together and bent to pick up a stone. She hurled it hard against the wooden fence of the house that backed onto the park. It ricocheted and landed at her mother's feet.

'Cut it out,' she said. They walked quietly for a moment. 'So who did you sit with?'

'By myself.'

Her mother raised her eyebrows.

'And some of the time with Sonya.'

'That's nice.'

'It's revolting.'

'You and Kim used to like playing with Sonya.'

'She's so childish. And she's always going on about secrets and when you ask her it's just something really boring that you know anyway.'

'Never mind. Maybe someone nice'll move into Kim's house. Someone with kids your age.'

Susie looked up at her. 'I know who's moving into Kim's house. She's a horrible old bag and she hasn't got any kids . . . and I hate her.'

'Susie! Don't you speak about anyone like that.'

They crossed Australia Street and went down the lane beside the panel beater's. They came out behind the Catholic church, cut through the children's playground and crossed the street to their gate. A letter with an airmail sticker poked out of the top of the letterbox. Susie's mother pulled it out and studied the stamps and then the address on the back.

Susie kicked the gate open and went up the steps. 'Who's it from?'

Her mother dropped the letter into her bag and pulled out her keys.

'Is that from my father?'

'Yes.'

'Aren't you going to read it?'

'When I get round to it.'

They went down the hall and into the kitchen. Susie turned on the radio and stood fiddling with the dial. Her mother filled the kettle.

'Crikey, turn that noise down!'

'It's not noise, it's music, and it's not too loud.'

'I say it is.'

'You can't do anything round this place.' Susie went into the next room and fell into a large armchair, her legs up and over the side.

'Haven't you got some homework or something to do on your project before tea?'

'Yeah, in a minute.' Susie rolled out of the chair, straightened up, and came back into the kitchen. She opened the fridge and took out the orange juice. She poured a drink, gulped it down and tossed the cup into the sink. She was halfway up the stairs when her mother called, 'By the way, Nina's coming for tea.'

'Yuk. Why does she have to come?'

'Because I want her to. Because she wants to. I thought you liked her.'

'Well you thought wrong. I hate her.'

'Suse!'

'Not really hate. But why does she always have to come?' She didn't wait for an answer, but stomped upstairs, bashing her bag against the banisters. She slammed the door of her bedroom, threw the bag against the far wall and slid into the desk chair. She picked up the photograph of her father from its place on top of some books. She looked hard at the neat, short hair, the serious face the dark suit coat. 'It was his passport photo,' her mother had told her. 'He never really looked like that.' *But what did he really look like? Who was he?* She turned the photograph face down and looked at her project book, open on the desk. Coloured pencils spilled across the blank title page. She moved them all to the floor and opened her homework folder.

*My Family*
*In my family there is just my mother and me. Her*
*name is Martha O'Neil and I am Susie. We live in*
*Macquarie Street, Newtown. She works at the*
*Hospital as a technician in a laboratory. Sometimes I*

*wish I had brothers and sisters like some other kids but other times its great being just me with Mum. When she gets cranky I'd like someone else! She doesn't get cranky too much. She doesn't have any brothers and sisters either so I haven't got any cousins. I used to have a Nanna but she died when I was six and the budgie died last year and we haven't got another one yet. Mum says I can get one at Xmas. I've got a father called Victor Simpson who used to live in Australia but now he lives in Italy and I don't know much about him.*

Susie ruled a straight line under the writing. Then she drew herself first, sitting at the kitchen table. She did her mother sitting opposite. The two figures were the same size so she rubbed herself out and started again, smaller. She stopped when Nina arrived.

The front door slammed and the two women went down the hall and into the kitchen. The tap was turned on, lids clanged against saucepans and there was the loud shriek of Nina laughing. Susie opened her door and listened.

'. . . in her room, doing her homework.'

'How is she with no Kim?'

'O.K. I think. She'll get over it. I don't want to make too big a deal of it.'

Susie pushed the spaghetti around her plate with the back of her fork.

'Salad?' said Nina. She passed the bowl across the table. The silver bangles she wore jangled on her wrist. She always wore silver, on her fingers, her ears, around her neck. There was a time when Susie was only six when she had even worn a silver chain with a tiny silver bell around her ankle. But not now. Nina ran her fingers through her short red hair and swung back in her chair so that it balanced on only two legs.

'So Kim's gone, has she?'

Susie nodded. She didn't look up. She concentrated on looping the last bit of spaghetti round the prongs of her fork. The thick tomato sauce dripped onto the white plate and she mopped it up with her bread. She could feel her mother looking carefully at her.

When the plate was clean, she had to look up at them.

Nina was leaning on her elbows on the table now, sipping a glass of wine and chuckling. 'You know, when I was about your age, no, I'd've been a bit older, about thirteen, my closest friend left town. I cried for a week.' She put the glass down. 'Within a fortnight, I'd fallen in love with the boy who sat behind me in maths and I'd almost completely forgotten her.' She looked at Susie's mother. 'You know I can't even remember his name now.' She laughed. 'He wore glasses and long shorts. Amazing what you get over when you're young.'

*Kim. Forgotten in a week!*

Susie pushed her chair back and jumped up.

'You might forget your friends in a week, but I won't.'

'Susie, sit down. Nina didn't mean it like that,' Her mother looked from one to the other.

'Yeah, I'm sorry. I didn't mean it to sound like that. Sit down.' Nina patted the table.

'Don't you tell me what to do. You're not my mother.'

'Suse!'

'And don't *you* call me Suse! I hate it and I hate you.' She kicked the chair over as she ran to the foot of the stairs. She stumbled slightly then picked herself up and pounded up to her room, slamming the door behind her. She fell across the room, onto her bed, cracking her ankle on the trundle-bed beneath hers. Kim's bed. Where she slept on the nights she stayed. Above her were the posters of Madonna and the Wham! concert that they hadn't been allowed to go to, Kim's presents on her twelfth birthday. The kite they made in art. *You do the drawing on it, Susie, you're good at that.* The long green tail of the kite hung from one corner of the ceiling to the other, stuck with Blu-Tack. On windy summer nights it fell down and trailed across Susie's shoulder as she sat at the desk. On the back of the door hung a shaggy black jacket. They'd bought it together for five dollars from the op shop in Enmore. *I'll wear it Monday to Wednesday and you wear it till Sunday.* And down the side of the window frame were the strips of crazy photos from the booth at Newtown station. Kim with her head on Susie's shoulder. Eyes popping. Laughing. Susie with her hands behind her head, fingers spread. Kim side-on, her thumb to her nose. Kim's chin resting on Susie's crown. The back of their heads, Kim's hair, long and black, Susie's short and straight, mouse-coloured.

Susie got up from the bed and went over to the open window. The night air was hot and still. The bright moon lit up the spire over the church. Opposite it was Kim's house. *Is the woman there already? Changing everything? Her things where Kim's used to be?* Susie grabbed the photographs from the window frame and held them for a moment. Then she dropped them onto the desk and fell back onto the bed. She brushed the laughing clown and the furry koala to the floor, drew her knees up and hugging the soft pillow, rolled over to stare at the wall.

# Chapter 2

Susie woke up the next morning still in her clothes. Her mother's lap robe lay across her legs. She rolled onto her back and tucked her arm behind her head. The curtain was half-drawn so that the sun came through in a long thin shaft of light.

*Day one, P.K. Post Kim.*

*Amazing what you get over when you're young.*

*What would Nina know.*

'Su-se.' Her mother called from the kitchen.

The fridge door slammed. Susie smelt toast, heard a knife clatter against a plate. Water was poured into the kettle and then the radio blared out the music that came before the morning news.

'Susie!'

Outside, a dog barked and a car door slammed. The engine started and then revved.

She kicked off the lap robe, pulled on shorts and a T-shirt and went downstairs.

'Will you do the shopping for me this morning?' said her mother. She stood in her nightie, leaning against the sink, a cup of black coffee in her hand. 'Nina didn't leave till some ungodly hour.'

'She still whingeing on about that bloke who dropped her?'

Her mother nodded. She raised her eyebrows. 'On and on and on. Drives me crazy. You'd think no one else in the world had ever been left before.'

Susie licked the honey from her fingers and didn't look up. 'Amazing what you don't get over when you're old,' she said.

Her mother stared at her. 'That's a pretty cruel thing to say.'

'What she said to me last night was pretty cruel too.'

There was silence between them for a moment.

'Look, let's drop the whole thing.'

'Well, it's true, Mum. She never talks to me properly. She treats me like a baby or as if I'm not even here.' Susie leant on her elbows, looking up at her mother.

'I'm sorry, Susie, you do have a point. She's just not very good with kids. But she is my friend.'

'Well, just don't expect me to like her, that's all.'

Her mother turned her back and rinsed her coffee mug in the sink. She wiped her hands on a tea towel and then said, 'Now that you've got that out of your system, will you do the shopping for me this morning?'

'O.K.' Susie got a glass of milk from the fridge and waited while her mother wrote a list.

'There's not much. Some meat, a few vegies and then some things from the deli. And get me the papers too.' She passed the list to her daughter. 'I've got a bit of stuff to do for work and then I'm going to have a really lazy afternoon. What are you going to do?' She smiled brightly. 'Are you going to see any of the kids? Sonya? Tanya?'

Susie shrugged. She picked up the list and her mother's purse.

'Dunno,' she said.

'Well, if you meet them up the street you can bring them back for a cool drink.'

Outside it was hot. The back of Susie's neck burned. She swung the string shopping bag at her side and it slapped against her bare leg.

Pete Watson from next door was lying in the gutter, half under his car.

She nodded to his mother who was leaning on the gate.

'Be a bit warm today, love,' the woman said.

'Yeah.' Susie swung the bag up and around her head and started to jog to the corner. She went across the street and around the high brick wall that the McGregors had built to keep out the noise. David Egan had written the names of all the kids in the street in black marking pen on the white paint: His name at the top and underneath it, hers, Susie O'Neil. Susie went on up the back lane to King Street.

Sonya Mitchell and her sister Lisa stood in front of the delicatessen, talking to a couple of the boys from Lisa's class in high school.

*Damn it.*

Susie ducked into the newsagent's. She didn't want to buy the papers first. They were heavy and awkward to carry and the magazine always fell out onto the footpath. She headed for the back of the shop, past the stationery and school supplies to the glossies and the Lotto counter.

*Dolly, True Confessions, True Love.*

She picked up the closest magazine and flicked it open.

TOO YOUNG TO KNOW

IN LOVE WITH MY TEACHER *(Yuk! Marsden!)*

WILL MY MOTHER EVER UNDERSTAND?

'Can I help you?' said a voice behind her. It was the newsagent, a tall thin man who stooped slightly and walked softly round the shop.

'No, thanks. I'm just looking.'

He half-turned away from her.

'It's not the public library, you know,' he sniffed.

Susie shoved the magazine back on the rack marked 'Knitting Patterns' and went to the front of the shop. She bumped into the stand of birthday cards. It spun for a moment and then, as she reached the door, crashed onto the pile of Saturday papers.

She giggled and walked quickly towards the deli, weaving to avoid the strollers and prams, the shopping trolleys and the people who stood talking or looking in the shop windows. She bought salami, cheese and fat black olives, paid her money and slipped the white paper parcels into the string bag.

'Next, please.'

'Susie!' Sonya faced her as she walked towards the door. 'It's really incredible. I was just talking about you . . . and here you are.' They left the shop together and stood outside.

'Look,' said Susie. 'I can't stop. I'm doing the shopping for Mum.'

'What about this afternoon?' said Sonya. 'Can you come over? I've got this really great secret to tell you. And new records. Lisa says we can play them.'

'I can't, Sonya. I have to go out with Mum. She says I have to.' Susie looked down at a crack in the footpath. Ants crawled over a torn ice-block wrapper. She kicked it into the gutter.

'Well, I'll tell you now anyway so you can ask her. It's Lisa's party. Mum says I can have some of our gang too. There's going to be boys and all there. Do you reckon she'll let you come?' Sonya leant forward. 'She will, won't she?'

Susie shrugged. 'I dunno. She's funny, sometimes.'
*She'll let me go, all right. Just what you need. Kim gone.*

15

*Get back in with the others in the gang. You used to be such
friends with them. Boys too. Yuk.*

'I've got to go,' said Susie. 'I said I'd be home. Mum'll
kill me if I'm late.'

'Well, ask her,' Sonya called, 'and I'll get my mum to
ring her up if she says no.'

Boys. Susie and Kim in the cemetery after school. Sneak
up behind the tomb with the anchor on the top. Watch
Martin Naylor and Cheryl Watson go behind the clump
of wattle trees. Stuff their fists in their mouths to stop
the giggles. Martin and Cheryl turn round. Hear only feet
racing along the gravel drive towards the gate.

Susie turned down the street at the side of the pub. The
shopping bag, heavy with meat and vegetables, fruit and
the things from the deli, bumped against her leg. She went
past the old School of Arts building, the furniture shop
and the back of the police station. She crossed the road
and went into the park beside the dry bed of roses. There
was no one around. She dropped the bag onto the grass
and lowered herself onto a swing, her arms draped loosely
around the chains. She kicked her thongs off and swayed
gently for a moment, her toe tracing a line in the dirt.
She stood up then and bent her knees into the movement
of the swing. She pushed her feet forward. Up. Back. Up
again. Hair falling back. Down again. Then up. Lying
almost flat. Air rushing past. And down.

She stood still on the swing, as it moved.

Across the park, against the wooden back fence of a house
on Australia Street, three old men sat and passed round
a flagon of wine. Their voices broke the hum of traffic
and from the corner of her eye, Susie caught the slow
movements of their arms.

The swing rocked gently.

Two small boys came running along the top of the cemetery wall. They breathed hard, laughing. Suddenly, the one at the front stopped and dropped down to sit astride the huge block of sandstone. He pointed into the cemetery and his friend leant forward, their heads almost touching.

'Witch, witch, you're a stupid bitch,' the first boy yelled and the second one covered his mouth, giggling.

'What'cha doing, witch?' the second boy screamed.

There was silence from the other side of the wall.

Susie's swing was still.

Susie and Kim, six years old, run along the wall, drop down behind the tall bamboo, watch her drawing. 'Let's chuck a rock at her,' says Kim, 'and then run as fast as we can.' The rock falls short and they run, but, just for a moment, Susie wants to see what it is, sketched on the paper.

The boys turned and faced the slippery dip and seesaw. They stretched their arms behind their backs.

'Astro Boy!' yelled the first and leapt onto the concrete path. The other followed him and landed hard on the edge of the rosebushes.

Susie picked up the shopping bag and started to walk around the wall to the cemetery gate. She passed a man and his baby son kicking a plastic ball to each other. The mother leant back against the wall in the sun and read the papers. Behind her scrawled in white paint was the message: JUST WHEN YOU THOUGHT YOU KNEW WHAT WAS GOING ON . . .

Susie stopped at the gate.

*I won't even come here.*

The sun was almost directly overhead, burning her

17

shoulders, every part of her skin. She squinted and put her hand up to shade her eyes. Opposite was Kim's. The upstairs verandah was glassed-in for Kim and Joanne's bedroom. You could sit on top of the old toybox and look straight into the middle of the huge Moreton Bay fig tree and across to the bottom window of the church steeple. On nights when Susie stayed the night, Joanne moved into the back bedroom and Susie and Kim sat and watched the people come home from King Street, holding onto the cemetery railings, leaning for a moment against the solid gate supports. They saw couples come out from behind the tree. They shivered and wondered if the Blue Lady was there too.

Susie moved through the gate into the shadow of the huge fig tree and leant against the roots that thrust themselves up from the gravelly soil.

# Chapter 3

Susie peered down the avenue of palms and bamboo. Nothing moved. She stepped out onto the path, the gravel crunching beneath her feet. Slowly past the church door, the monument to the bishops, the slab that marked the distance to the city.

*I won't even come here.*

She turned off the path and ducked beneath the low branches of an oak tree. She heard a rustling sound, grass moving, caught a glimpse of blue against the gold sandstone wall. She crouched low behind a headstone.

*She's in Kim's house.*

Susie gripped the grave's rusted iron railing till the brown powder came off on her skin.

*If it wasn't for her, Kim would've stayed.*

A tiny pink rosebud touched against her cheek. She brushed it aside and when it sprang back against her she grabbed it wildly and crushed the petals. A thorn dug into her palm and she fought back tears as she pulled it out.

*If it wasn't for her this wouldn't have happened.*

Susie worked her way forward, half-crawling, out across an open space and then she hid behind a thick palm tree. The woman didn't look up. She sat with her back to the wall, a pad of paper on her knees. Thick grey hair fell over her shoulders and across her face. She brushed it back with one hand while she went on sketching. At her feet was a battered brown felt hat with a red feather stuck in the band.

'But what d'you reckon she's drawing?' Susie asks Kim the first time they notice her.
    'I don't know and I don't care.'
    Susie never asks again.

The woman looked up for a moment. She scratched the side of her head with the end of her pencil, turned the page of the drawing pad and started again.
    *What's she drawing? People don't just draw. Kids do at school, and art teachers. And me when I'm at home, in my room, by myself.*
    'You draw so well,' Susie's mother says to her when she looks at her project book. 'You must get it from your father. I can't draw for nuts.'

The woman stood up. She dropped the pad and pencil into a large pocket in her skirt, picked up the shopping trolley at her feet and walked towards the place where Susie hid.
    Susie looked around quickly. To one side of her was a clump of trees whose branches trailed almost to the ground. The woman stopped. She bent down and picked something up from the grass. Susie ran, stumbled over a bag of rubbish, ducked behind the drooping branches, and watched as the woman reached a sunken headstone. She took a small kitchen knife from her other pocket and scraped at the far side of the stone block. Something came away in her hand and she dropped it into the shopping trolley. She sat down on the slab and flapped her skirt to cool her legs. Then she fanned her face with the hat and squashed it firmly on her head, tying the dangling strings beneath her chin. Susie was close enough to see

the patchy brown freckles on her hands and the deep wrinkles on her cheek. Her faded blue blouse was crumpled and a seam was coming apart under her arm. She tipped the trolley up and grass and leaves spilled at her feet. She bent forward and began to sort everything into piles. Her lips moved.

'You lot go over there. That's right. No. Not you. You're a ring-in . . .' There were green and yellow stains on her long thin fingers and the nails were cut right down.

Susie could barely catch the words.

The woman picked up a twig with the leaves still attached and turned it over carefully. 'Not you either. You'll just muck it all up.' She tossed the bits of leaf aside.

They always watch. 'She's making witches' brew,' says Kim.

'Budgie food, more likely,' says Susie. 'And David reckons talking to yourself is the first sign of madness.'

Susie looked around. Inside her curtain of branches was a heavy white slab and upright headstone. Pale green ferns and darker morning glory grew in the shadows. She lifted some of the creeper with her foot. A tiny lizard darted away. Two snails retreated into their shells. She picked them up and put them on the middle of the slab. . . . *remember the stew we made . . . slugs and snails and . . .* Quietly she pulled back the ferns and plucked three more snails from the ridges made by the worn writing at the base of the headstone.

AND OF HIS DAUGHTER, ELIZA EMILY DONNITHORNE. DIED 20TH MAY 1866.

Susie pulled carefully at the bag of rubbish. It fell open and four empty cans of cat food rolled away from her. She picked one up and began to drop the snails into it. She crushed leaves and a couple of the rich purple flowers and dropped them in too. She searched around the headstone and added broken glass, a Crunchie bar wrapper, a grey feather and the body of a cockroach, eaten away by the ants. She peered back through the branches.

The woman had packed the leaves and grasses into different plastic bags and was stuffing them back into the trolley. She stood up then, leaning on the metal handle as she straightened her back. She walked away, the trolley rattling behind her.

*Back to the house. Her house. Kim's house.*

But then she left the path and went across the clearing towards the place where Kim and Susie played. Susie grabbed the can and spat into it. She left her shopping on the grass and ran along the gravel path.

Two old women, dressed as if they were going to church, their handbags clutched to their sides, stepped out of her way. They carried umbrellas against the sun and one had the guidebook to the cemetery.

The snails rattled in the tin.

*We should have dumped the lot on her.*

There was a line of cars moving slowly down Church Street. Susie glanced back over her shoulder.

*Hurry up. She'll come.*

At a break in the traffic, she darted across the road, pushed open the gate and ran up the front steps of Kim's house.

*Here's a letter from Kim. Special delivery.*

She giggled. Two of the snails had crawled up the inside of the can and were balanced on the edge. Susie picked them off and pushed them through the letterbox in the front door. Then she held the flap open and shook the can against it. She wanted to yell something as she heard the contents hitting the floor inside but it all happened so quickly and she couldn't think of anything. She ran back out onto the footpath and dropped the can. It bounced and clanged against the gutter as she raced across the road and through the cemetery gates.

Susie picked up her shopping bag, slung it over her shoulder and headed through the trees.

*Serve her right. Old bag.*

The two women, the guidebook held out in front of them, came towards her.

'Excuse me, dear,' said one. 'We're looking for the place where they buried the bodies from the shipwreck, the *Dunbar*, the famous one.'

Susie waved her hand towards the far southern corner.

'It's down there,' she said. 'Where the wall juts out.'

'And the other one we can't find,' said the woman, 'is Eliza Donnithorne. You don't know where she is, do you?'

'Donnithorne?'

*Why her? Was she famous?*

'She's in the trees,' said Susie. 'Down there. It's her father's really and she's at the bottom of the stone.' She stood watching as the women went along the path, stopping every couple of metres to read the names and inscriptions. When she turned back to walk down the path the Blue Lady was sitting at the base of the huge tree near the gate drawing.

Susie stopped and sat down on the grassy mound opposite the church door. She took an apricot out of the shopping bag and bit into it.

*Leave. Walk out straight past her. She won't say anything.*

She didn't move. She looked out over the cemetery wall to the red-roofed houses of Camperdown and Annandale. Far beyond them was the bush north of the city. She heard the thud of the seesaw and a woman's voice yelling, 'Come on, Scott! I'm leaving. Right now. I mean it.'

*Stand up. She doesn't know anything yet. Kim would just leave. We'd leave together. Kim would make me.*

Susie stood up. She finished the fruit and hurled the stone at the grave where she and Kim always played. It bounced off the upright and into the grass. She walked over to the huge sandstone block and ran her hand along the smooth slab. Nothing had changed. It was at the highest point in the cemetery, hidden from the street by the oak trees and thickly planted gums. Kim had found the secret postbox, swinging on the prow of the ship one day. It had slid away under her weight and at first she thought she had broken it and had leapt down, ready to run. But it was how it was meant to be. A place to hide things that no one else knew.

Susie tugged at the jutting piece of stone. It moved sideways and she felt behind it. There was something there! Paper. A note. Susie snatched it out and spun round in the sunshine. There was no writing. It was a pencil drawing. She spread it on the headstone and bent over it. It was her. Them. Susie and Kim. They were leaning against the headstone. Kim was looking down at Susie as she always did when she planned things, worked out where they'd go, what they'd do. Susie grinned up at her in the glare. The freckles were right. The bit of hair was there— the one that she plastered with water to stop it from sticking out. It still did, no matter what. And Kim. It was just like Kim. Where had it come from? Who had left it for her to find?

Susie picked up the drawing and looked down through the trees towards the street. Yesterday the postbox had been empty. Kim was in Melbourne. It had to be someone who could draw, who saw them, watched them in the

24

cemetery. Someone who *knew* them. She shivered.

The Blue Lady had gone.

Susie walked slowly down the path to the gate, then she stood and stared across at the closed door of Kim's house.

# Chapter 4

Susie was hungry. She ran as fast as she could across the park, leaping over the cracks in the cement. The shopping bag bounced against her back.

David came towards her on his bike. He did a huge wheelie on the grass and came alongside. She kept on running.

'Where've you been?'

'Nowhere.'

'You're going to cop it when your mum gets you.'

He grinned. He lived at the back and if he climbed the apricot tree in the corner of his yard, he could talk to Susie as she sat at her bedroom window. Susie looked at him out of the corner of her eye. She stopped, hands on hips, bending forward and taking in great gulps of air. 'What do you mean?' she said.

'I just saw her at Maria's shop. She wanted to know if I'd seen you. Reckons you went out ages ago.'

*I've been in the park, Mum. I couldn't leave. Don't ask me why.*

Susie walked with David riding slowly beside her. She felt the drawing, tucked inside her T-shirt, scratch her bare skin.

*Snails slide and squelch on the cold floor.*

Susie shuddered. 'I've just been hanging around,' she said.

At the end of the park, David rode off.

'See ya.'

Susie waved.

He's so childish, says Kim. But Kim is gone.

The door was open. Susie went down the hall, slowly. She tossed the shopping onto the kitchen table and rubbed her hands together. 'What's for lunch, Mum? I'm starving.'

Her mother turned from the sink and dried her hands on her jeans. She arched an eyebrow. 'The usual Saturday help-yourself . . . And where have you been, young lady?'

Susie opened the fridge and took out juice, bread, butter, and left-over salad. She spread the things along the bench and then bent to get a glass from the cupboard.

'I asked you, Susie, where you've been for the last couple of hours.'

'I heard you, Mum. Hang on a minute.'

'I will not hang on a minute. You don't need to be fed to answer a simple question.'

Susie started to butter a slice of bread. 'Well,' she spoke slowly and didn't look up at her mother, 'I did the shopping and I ran into Sonya . . . and you're always going on about how you reckon I don't spend enough time with the kids . . . so . . .'

'Sonya's mother rang me over an hour ago when Sonya got home. I assumed you'd be home soon after.' Her mother stood in the middle of the kitchen, her hands full of plates to be put away, looking across at Susie. 'She asked me if you could go to Lisa's party. I said yes but now I'm not so sure I'll let you go.'

*Good. I don't want to go.*

Susie looked down. 'I went to the park and played on the swings and stuff.'

'For an hour?'

'Yes, for an hour.' Susie shrugged. Then she almost

27

mumbled, 'And for some of that time I was in the cemetery.'

'Su-se.'

'Don't call me that.'

'I'll call you what I like. You know I've told you a thousand times I do not like you going into that place, especially on your own.'

'I wasn't the only one there.' She put lettuce and tomato on the bread.

'Who were you with then?' Her mother put her hand on Susie's shoulder and spun her around. 'Who?'

'Nobody. It was just this lady. And I wasn't *with* her. I was watching her. You wouldn't know her.'

'Who is she? How do you know I wouldn't know her?'

Her mother's fingernails pressed against the soft skin of her shoulder. Susie shook herself free. 'She's the old bat I told you about. The one in Kim's house. The Blue Lady. That's what Kim and I call her. The little kids reckon she's a witch but they're stupid.'

'The Blue Lady?' Her mother leant back against the fridge. She wrinkled her forehead.

'She just always wears blue.' Susie shrugged. 'She's living in Kim's house now, but she's always around, in the cemetery. She draws all the time.'

'Do you talk to her?'

'No way.'

Her mother dropped her hands to her sides, turned and went out to the laundry. Susie went back to making her sandwich. Her mother came into the kitchen, the orange plastic washing basket on her hip.

'Come out in the sun,' she said. 'I haven't finished talking.'

Susie sat on the back step and watched her mother bend and stretch from the basket to the line. A slight breeze flapped the wet clothes against her skin. At each bend, her hair fell into her eyes and as she stood up, she tucked it back behind her ears.

'Don't you trust me, Mum?' said Susie.

'It's not that I don't trust you,' said her mother. 'It's just that . . . Well, you're only twelve. There're some pretty weird people around. I just worry a bit. There have been bashings and everything in that park. And, if you ask me, that cemetery is an even more ideal place for things to happen. So I don't want you going in there again, right? You meet your friends out in the open where there are lots of others.'

She bent and picked up a pair of Susie's jeans. She pegged them on the line and then shook the legs till they hung down, straight.

Susie finished her sandwich and licked the last tomato seed off her fingers.

'Is she an artist?' Her mother started hanging out the wet tea towels.

Susie shrugged. 'I don't know. Kim hates her because she's got their house. She reckons she's crazy 'cause she talks to herself.'

*I hate her too . . . But the drawing . . .*

'How would she know, Susie? Or you for that matter? You're just a kid. You know nothing about the way some people can be.' Her mother shook her head and picked up the basket. 'So she's an old woman?'

'Older than you. More like Mrs Watson.' Susie grinned.

Her mother went inside.

Susie sat, staring at the white brick fence.

'It's like in Greece,' Nina had said. She came for lunch three summers ago, on a Saturday, with huge cans of paint. Susie and Kim put on their swimming costumes and beach hats and painted all day. David sat in the fork of the apricot

29

tree at the end of his yard so he could look right down on top of them. He went to the shop for his mother and when he got back he came and painted too. They did the whole wall, twice, and now it was covered with a huge shiny green vine of passionfruit and a pink geranium.

'You're not listening to me, Susie.'

'What?' Susie looked back into the darkened laundry. 'Sorry, I was thinking about the day we painted the fence.' The spots of paint were still on her old navy blue swimming costume.

'I said I felt like going for a swim. Why don't you get your togs and come?'

'To the pool at work?'

Her mother nodded.

'O.K.'

They swam lengths in the tiny pool behind the nurses' home. Freestyle, up and down ten times. Then breaststroke.

'I like coming here.' Susie grinned and spat out the water between her teeth.

Her mother looked curiously at her.

' 'Cause no one from school can see us and say what a dag for going swimming with your mum.' She rolled sideways and swung her arms to throw water high in the air.

Her mother sprinted towards her and ducked her hard, twice. They both came up laughing. They did duck-dives and somersaults. Susie tried to do a figure-of-eight. Then her mother showed her how to turn, underwater at the lowest part. They practised together for a bit and then she said, 'Have you got the hang of it?'

Susie nodded, grabbed a breath and duck-dived again.

Her mother got out and lay in the shade with a book while Susie practised . . . forward and down till almost at the bottom of the pool . . . roll over and flick your wrists till you come up into the sun, on your back . . . legs behind, head down forward and . . .

When she finally got out, the skin on her fingers was wrinkled. She shook her hair over her mother's back and then flopped down beside her.

'Mum.'

'Mmmm.'

'Why did he write that letter, yesterday? He never writes.'

Her mother lifted her head slightly. She hesitated and kept her eyes on the page. She wasn't reading. 'No real reason. He just wanted to.'

'What did he say?'

'Nothing much. Just news about people you don't know. The weather. Things like that. Apparently the fog has come down in Milan. It's wet and freezing.'

'I thought Italy was sunny.'

'Some parts. Sometimes.' Her mother rolled onto her back. 'Why do you want to know?'

Susie shrugged. 'He is my father.'

'Not that he's done much about it.' She stood up and slipped her feet into thongs and pulled a long T-shirt over her head. 'Come on. Let's go home and get a drink.'

They walked out of the sunlight, down the cool, dark hallway. They poured cold drinks and sipped them slowly. 'For the rest of the afternoon,' said Susie's mother, 'I am going to sit out the back and read the papers.'

Susie pulled a face . . .

'You didn't forget them? God, Susie! I don't ask you to do much.' She dropped her glass into the sink. 'I'll get changed and go myself. I suppose they'll be closed now and I'll have to go up and get them at the café.' She disappeared into the bathroom.

Susie went upstairs. She lay on the floor in her swimming costume and pulled her photo album down from the bookshelf. It started with kindergarten. Somewhere was a baby book with the earlier pictures. She opened it at the first page. Toothless grins. Susie in skimpy cotton dresses, in shorts and a T-shirt, her schoolbag on her back, balancing on the fence with David. Then in first class, with Kim. At the beach, at the pool, on the swings. Running, swimming. Scabby knees and summer freckles. They sit together in stiff class photographs. Arms around each other to blow out candles. Joint party for birthdays a week apart. Dressed in Bib and Bub costumes for their first fancy dress party. Legs grow longer. Baggy sweaters with bright paintings and rock band logos. Kim with a bra and pierced ears.

Susie rolled onto her back.

The front door slammed.

She stared at the paper lightshade till its edges blurred against the flaking paint of the ceiling. The tail of the kite looked for a moment as if it would fall loose. It quivered above her in the slightest of breezes then hung perfectly still.

# Chapter 5

'Got a letter from Kim yet?' Cheryl walked with Susie across the playground. Tanya and Sonya raced ahead to grab the bench under the jacaranda tree.

Susie rubbed her apple against her skirt and bit into it. 'Not yet,' she said. 'She's only been gone a week.'

Two fifth class kids were playing nudging right in front of the bench.

'Watch out,' said Cheryl.

They each kept holding tightly to one foot. Shoulders dropped, they hopped towards each other, bobbing, almost dancing then charging forwards and crashing together. One stumbled and fell back against Susie who slipped and fell over.

'Clear out!' she yelled. 'Get over in your own space.' She stood up and picked the bits of gravel and tar out of the graze on her leg. 'They're so childish!'

Cheryl nodded, 'Yeah.'

They slid in next to Tanya and Michelle. Sonya was talking to Tracey behind the tree. 'Some secret conversation,' said Michelle tossing her head in their direction. 'Probably just the party and we all know about it anyway.'

'You allowed to go?' said Susie.

Michelle nodded. Tanya grinned. 'It's going to be unreal,' she said.

' 've you got a letter yet?' Tracey slid along the bench to join Susie.

'Nope.'

'She's probably having too good a time with that cousin of hers and the spunky boyfriend.' Tanya leant forward as Sonya sat down. 'What's Lisa got planned for us at the party, eh?'

Sonya pulled a piece of paper from her pocket and spread it on the table. The others crowded forward to see. She picked the paper up again and held it close to her chest. 'Hang on. Just hang on a sec.' She looked at them, making them wait for her next words 'Lisa says that if we're all going to come, we have to do what she says and not wreck her party. She's got everything arranged. I've got the lists and I have to tell you now what you have to do.'

Susie kept munching her apple. She flicked the blue jacaranda flowers from the table and scratched at the splintery wood.

'Are we going to play spotlight?' Tanya giggled and nudged Michelle.

'Preferably without the spot.' Michelle giggled back.

'Without the light, you mean.'

'It's like that,' said Sonya. 'You all get a number and you have to draw another number out of a hat.' She shrugged. 'Or a box or something. Then you have to go up the back with the boy who's got that number. It'll be really dark and you have to kiss him and we have to count how long you are.' She smirked.

'What if you don't like him?'

*Kiss him. Yuk.*

'Yeah, what if he's got pimples and stinks like Geoffrey Meaney?'

34

Susie bit into a bruised, bad part of her apple. She spat the brown mouthful onto the ground.

*Kissing. Only with Mum and that's on the cheek. She always smells warm.*

'You've all got to play.' Sonya waved her piece of paper. 'And if he's pimply and stinks, it doesn't matter. It'll be dark and you don't have to look at him.'

'Put a peg on your nose,' said Michelle.

'And anyway,' said Sonya, 'Lisa's got it all worked out so you know who it is that you're going to have.'

'I thought it came out of a hat?'

'Only sort of.' Sonya giggled. 'We know but they don't.'

She spread her sheet on the table and Tanya, Tammy, Michelle and Cheryl bent forward to check it.

A tennis ball flew past them and hit the fence. Susie got up and went over to get it. She threw it hard, back to the group of little kids on the far side of the playground. They scrambled to catch it.

*What if the boy thought, yuk!? If he thought you were a dag? That you smelt? If he pulled a face when he saw who he'd got, and refused to go?*

*Would he know you'd never kissed a boy before?*

*If he did know, would he tell?*

'Come here and have a look, Susie.' Sonya pointed to the sheet. 'See. Tanya gets Nick Soulos, Cheryl gets Peter Williams, Michelle gets Scotty, I'm going to have Brett Nichols, Tracey gets Michael Zazzi and you get Tom Dogget.'

'Dogget? Who's he?'

'Sounds like Dog Turd,' Tanya giggled.

*Trust Tanya to get Nick. Biggest spunk in sixth class last year. And smart.*

'Are you going with Nick?' Cheryl asked Tanya.

'Not yet.'

Susie tossed her apple core into the bin. 'If your sister thinks I'm kissing a dog turd, she can think again.'

*What would Kim say? What would she do?*

'Don't you wreck our party, Susie O'Neil.' Sonya stood up and looked at all of them. 'Lisa'll kill me if we don't do it.'

'Anyway,' said Susie, 'I mightn't be allowed to go yet. Mum's been going off her brain all week.'

'How come? What'd you do?'

'Nothing. Just the usual. Nah, nah, your room's a mess.' She was standing apart from the group, one hand on her hip, the fingers of her other hand pointing the way her mother did when she came into her room and couldn't see the carpet for clothes. 'Your music's too loud. This isn't a hotel I'm running.' She flopped down on the seat beside Michelle.

'That's not enough to stop you going to a party.'

'You don't know my mum.'

At three twenty-five, Susie stood at the lights at King Street. She watched the huge semi-trailers roar past, her eyes level with the top of their wheels. They grunted and slowed as the lights changed.

Michelle raced up and joined her as she started to cross. She was puffing in the heat and gasped as she talked.

' 's gonna be really great. Mum says I can get a new pair of jeans and top . . . What you wearing?'

Susie shrugged. 'Dunno. Like I said, I mightn't be going.'

'She'll let you, won't she?'

'Dunno.'

'Look!' Michelle stopped outside the jeans shop. She pointed to a tall thin model wearing skin-tight navy jeans, a wide leather belt and a baggy shirt.

'That's what I'm getting.' She pressed her nose against the glass. She wasn't as tall as the model's shoulder. 'D'you like it?'

'Looks good on her,' said Susie. She leant against the window. 'Who'd you draw in the game, again?'

'Darren Scott.' She looked down.

'Oh, that's right. Are you going to kiss him?'

'We have to.'

'Well, I'm not kissing Tom What's-'is-name.'

'Are you going to miss the party?' Michelle and Susie walked towards the next corner. 'He might be a real spunk.'

'A real dag, you mean. If he was anything great, Lisa'd keep him for herself—or for one of her friends.' She swung her bag up and over her shoulder. 'I'll think of something. But don't you tell.'

Michelle crossed King Street, waving to Susie as she got caught up in kids and shoppers. Susie waited for a moment, looking into the window of the Lebanese cake shop, then she stepped out into the side road. She dodged the cars and a bread van, reached the other footpath and headed towards the cool of the park and the cemetery.

The man from the gatehouse was slashing grass near his front fence. He waved and kept working. Susie didn't follow the path that she and Kim always took. Instead she skirted the main area and went across to where she could climb up on the wall between the park and the cemetery. She dragged her schoolbag up beside her and sat astride the hot stone, her back to the street and Kim's house.

There were kids playing cricket in the park. David was fielding close to where Susie sat. The ball came in his direction. He missed and it smacked into the wall. He threw it back and then stayed, leaning against the stone near Susie's feet.

'D'you want to play?' he said.

She shook her head.

'You can have a bat.' He scratched at a gap between two stones and didn't look at her. 'And you can have a bowl, too.'

'No,' she said 'I don't feel like it.' She stood up and started to walk along the top of the wall, glancing over to the cemetery side, looking for a good place to jump.

'What are you doing in there, anyway? You're just stuck-up,' David yelled at her and he ran back to the game.

'I am not.'

*What are you doing in there?*

Susie jumped down onto a mound of earth and ran across the cemetery towards the area where she and Kim played.

*What are you doing in there?*

She ran through the grove of palm trees and under the bamboo, tall as the church roof.

*What are you doing in there?*

She ran past the anchor, past the grave of all the kids who had the fever, past the stones that had fallen and lay broken in the grass, till she reached the headstone of the boy who had died at sea.

*I want to know why she drew us . . . I want to ask her . . . I'm sorry . . . for the snails.*

She sat puffing, her head forward on her knees. She clenched her fist.

*I am not sorry . . . I hate her, hate her.*

She looked up. A blue skirt disappeared behind the tall orange flowering gum tree and went along the path towards the gate.

She stood up and stared after the woman. Then she turned back to the headstone. The prow of the boat seemed to jut out at a strange angle. Susie walked slowly around it. She reached out and touched it.

*Don't be silly. There'll be nothing.*

*No letter. No drawing.*

She listened to the magpies, high above the bamboo. She tugged at the stone. It gave. She reached in. Nothing. Cold, empty stone. She pushed her hand right to the back of the space. It touched the edge of a piece of paper. She lifted it out carefully. It was thin, white paper. She spread it on the grass and crouched over it. This time, drawn on it in black pen and ink was a single face. Her face, with freckles and sticking-out hair and eyes that looked away.

Susie sat at her desk, pen in hand and writing paper in front of her.

*Dear Kim . . . I miss you and wish you would come back to school . . .*

*Dear Kim . . . School's horrible, Mum goes off her brain all the time and I wish you'd never left . . .*

*Dear Kim . . . You know the crazy Blue Lady . . .*

The drawing was in the box under the bed. Susie had put it there with the other one, on top of the postcard from Kim's last holiday in Queensland. Kim's letters would go there too.

*Why hadn't she written and sent an address?*

Susie doodled in wide sweeping lines. It turned into a huge snail, that filled the page with its swirling shell. She giggled, then blushed and ripped the page from the writing pad and tossed it across the room. She leant forward and pushed the window up higher. From the backyard came the voices of her mother and Mrs Watson. Susie stood on tiptoe and leant across the desk to peer out.

'. . . it's Suse I'm a bit worried about,' said her mother.

39

She was balancing on top of a couple of bricks so that her head came just to the top of the fence.

'She's on her own a lot now that that friend of hers has gone. And she keeps on talking about an old woman who's up in the cemetery a fair bit. Suse says she's always drawing. She seems harmless enough but I don't really like it . . .'

Her voice dropped away and Susie didn't hear what she said next.

'. . . Jess,' said Mrs Watson. 'She's been back a good while now.' She leant forward and rested both elbows on the fence. 'She grew up round here. Mind you, she's a few years older than me. A bit funny, they say.' She tapped the side of her head with one finger. 'She wouldn't hurt a fly, though. You know, she went away for years and years. She was going to get married to this bloke. All of a sudden, the wedding was off, the actual day it was supposed to happen. It was a great drama. I knew because my sister was friendly with a friend of the bloke that she was getting married to. They couldn't tell all the guests in time so people kept arriving at the church to find out the wedding was off, he'd jilted her and she'd disappeared. Imagine that. Deserted on the very day. Broken heart, I suppose. 'Course it didn't seem to worry him too much. He married someone else six months later. They had the pub down Enmore Road. He died a while back. Anyhow, no one saw hide nor hair of her for years, all through the war, and after. Then, blow me down, if I didn't see her myself, on King Street about five years ago. I hardly recognised her. Peg, you know Peg from down the road, she was with me. We nearly died. I've seen her a few times since.' She stood back a bit from the fence. 'I wouldn't worry about her. Like I said, she's just a bit funny. Poor old thing. Never married, I imagine.'

40

Susie's mother didn't say anything. Mrs Watson raised her eyebrows.

'Oh, well,' she said, 'I suppose I'd better go in and get Stan and Pete's tea ready. They like it to be on the table when they get in the door.'

# Chapter 6

'I want you to promise me something, Suse.'

Susie looked up from her toast.

'I want you to go to Sonya's after school, or Michelle's, but you are not to go near that cemetery.' Her mother poured a glass of orange juice and slid it across the table. 'I worry about it and I'd feel better if you'd just promise me.'

'Sonya's boring.'

'She might be organising stuff for the party. You could help.'

Susie sipped the juice slowly.

*Help write names for the game. Susie O'Neil. Tom Dogget. I don't want to go, Mum. I'm scared. Don't make me.*

She coughed and took another piece of toast and spread it with Vegemite.

Her mother got up and went across to the sink. She turned the taps on to start the washing up and then half-turned to Susie and said, 'I asked Betty next door about your old woman.'

'She's not my old woman.'

*But she drew me. Why?*

'You know who I mean.' Her mother squirted in the detergent and slid the plates and cups into the water. 'Seems she used to live round here and she got jilted at the altar, you know, the wedding was called off, and she cleared out. Betty reckons it made her a bit funny. Though mind you, I got the feeling that Betty didn't know the full story. Anyway, you should feel sorry for the poor old thing.'

'Well, I don't.' Susie finished her drink and took the glass across to her mother. 'She's in Kim's house. She's probably changed everything. I bet she's even sleeping in Kim's room.'

'Susie, if it wasn't her it would be someone else. Kim's gone and that had nothing to do with your Blue Lady. She left because her dad got a job in Melbourne. It's as simple as that.' Susie's mother let the water out and dried her hands. 'Just remember what I said. No going there this afternoon.'

The last lesson of the day was art.

'Give me a hand with these brushes,' Mrs Chamberlain said to Susie as she hung the last of the paintings up to dry. Susie watched Sonya and Michelle leave.

'How are things without Kim?' said Mrs Chamberlain.

'O.K.'

'Have you heard from her?'

'Not yet.'

No letters. She ran to the box every day. Nothing from Melbourne. Her mother was looking too. Only bills, circulars and an early Christmas card from her mother's friend George who lived in California.

'You'll probably hear from her when the holidays start. She must be busy settling in.' Mrs Chamberlain shut the cupboard and walked back to her desk.

'Your work's not suffering. That painting you did was excellent. You do like painting, don't you?'

Susie nodded.

43

*Tell her about the Blue Lady. Show her the drawings. She draws too. She'd understand.*

'Well, I think you should consider doing art all the way through high school. You've got a lot of talent and there are so many different things you could do with it — not just drawing and painting but things with clay and fabric.' She picked up her books and they walked to the door. 'I'd be happy to talk to your mum if she wants me to.'

'Thanks.' Susie hesitated for a moment.

'Is there something you wanted to ask me?'

'No, nothing. See you.' Susie ran across the empty playground to the back lane and out into the traffic.

She walked slowly along King Street. The front door key lay in her pocket. At home was the project, set by Mr Marsden at the beginning of term. She had worked on it with Kim till all that was left to do were the headings and a couple of pictures. She could finish it this afternoon. Or there was always the library. In the wintertime, she and Kim climbed the stairs beside the old hall and sat around the worktable in the stuffy room. They left their homework aside and found magazines where girls wore black or red leather clothes and high plastic boots and had their hair cut long on one side and shaved on the other.

She stopped in front of the first of the second-hand shops. In the window stood a model, head thrown back, one hand on her hip, the other stuck out, trailing bright red beads. Her hair was long and thick and she had a serious look on her face, but there was a chip out of her plaster cheek and one foot was missing. The end of the beads rested on a china plate which had in its centre a picture of the wedding of Prince Charles and Lady Di. The bride was sitting down, looking up at her new husband.

44

*How would she have felt if he'd jilted her? Would she have gone a bit funny?*

She giggled, then caught sight of herself in the mirror behind the model. She threw her head back and put her hand on her hip. The woman from the hairdresser's walked past behind her and frowned. Other faces passed quickly. She watched them in the mirror. Then eyes — blue eyes beneath long black lashes. A wrinkled brown face. A broad black straw hat with a wide blue ribbon trailing over her shoulders. The eyes met hers and then were gone. Susie spun round. The woman in the blue skirt was already past the butcher, jostled by shoppers, down near the Lebanese cake shop. Her trolley bumped along behind her.

Susie ran, keeping her in sight, past the newsagent's and the hot bread shop. The woman turned right into Church Street. Susie ducked down the first lane and ran as fast as she could along the narrow footpath. She crossed the children's playground and waved to David's little sister, Brooke, who was sitting on the swing. Brooke called her: 'D'you wanna play?'

'No, I'm busy.' Susie slowed down, puffing, and crossed the road to the gates of the church.

The Blue Lady was already at the doctor's corner. She paused for a moment and leant on the handle of her trolley. Susie ducked behind the sandstone gatepost. She watched the woman coming slowly down the street. The Blue Lady didn't grin and nod to people the way that Susie's mother did. When she passed the house where Debbie Martin's grandmother was watering her pot plants, she didn't look sideways even though old Mrs Martin stared at her.

*Did she know her from before? Before the war?*

The Blue Lady walked on, her hair, caught in a bun, bouncing against her neck. She wore flat sandals and her skirt came down well below her knees. She seemed smaller than Susie remembered. When she got to Kim's house she dragged the trolley behind her up the steps, opened the door and went in without looking round.

Susie went back along the path to the tree and climbed onto the broad, high roots. She dropped her schoolbag and swung herself up into the lower branches. She chose one that reached out over the fence. It was as wide as the cemetery wall and she sat astride it and pulled herself along. The tree was so solid that her movements barely caused a rustling of the leaves. She could see the woman moving around in the upstairs room across the road, her shadow against the glass of the double doors.

*Open the doors. Let me see in.*

But the blurred shape crossed and re-crossed the room, always back away from the glass.

Susie looked around. The doors of the church were shut. There was no one in the grounds. She leant against a fork in the branch and closed her eyes.

*The wedding guests arrive . . . Women in dresses below their knees and hats that half-shade their faces . . . Men in baggy suits and hats. They walk up to the door . . . Wait in small groups . . . Whisper to each other . . . Wonder where . . .*

A door slammed. The Blue Lady came across the road and into the cemetery. She walked right beneath the branch where Susie sat. Susie held her breath, but the woman didn't look up. She went down the gravel path and disappeared behind the Chinese elms. Susie turned and looked after her.

*Jump down. Follow her. Ask her why . . . Say . . .*

Susie scratched at the bark of the branch. There was a crunching of shoes on the gravel and the woman reappeared. Again Susie held her breath.

*Don't look up.*

The woman carried a handful of grass and leaves. She left the cemetery and quickly crossed the street and went inside.

Susie pushed her way back along the branch and slid down the trunk.

She straightened her clothes, picked up her bag and stood for a moment, looking across at the paint peeling off the closed-in verandah and the drawn curtains.

*There were blinds before. Plain white blinds that you pulled down and then let spring back. They were there yesterday. What else was changed?*

Susie crossed the road and looked over the fence. The blinds, the old carpet from the upstairs landing and three bulging garbage bags were stacked against the bricks.

She walked up to the corner, and went round to the back lane. Kim's house had a back gate but you couldn't open it from the outside. There was a derelict house across the lane. The fence was down and just inside was a jacaranda. Its branches spread wide and touched the top of the outside toilet in Kim's yard. The blue flowers fell in early summer and got trodden into the cracked concrete.

Susie left her bag at the foot of the tree and began to climb. It was harder than the one in the churchyard. Spiky sticks scratched her arms and legs. Her knees hurt as she dragged herself up the first part of the trunk to one of the outstretched branches. As she worked her way along it, it dipped and rested heavily on the toilet roof. The backyard was empty. Susie reached out till her foot touched the top of the fence. She swung herself forward, balanced on the fence rail and then dropped to the ground, hidden from the house by the open toilet door.

Susie ran across the yard and ducked behind the laundry. There was no one at the window of the kitchen.

Nothing in the backyard had changed. She crouched down beside a pile of broken bricks and flower pots. The mint bush still grew under the leaking downpipe from the upstairs bathroom. She knew the back of the house well. When she and Kim played hide-and-seek, she rolled herself into a tight ball and curled up inside the old copper. It sat unused beside the white washing machine. There were cement tubs there as well, beneath shelves, heavy with soap and washing powder, insect sprays and empty paint cans.

Susie pressed her face to the laundry window, then pulled back quickly. The Blue Lady was there, bent over the steaming copper, stirring with a long wooden stick. Susie leant against the wall. She could feel her heart thumping.

*Spells. Magic. Don't be stupid.*

She breathed slowly and turned back to the window. As she watched, the woman hooked something from the copper and lifted it up. Water streamed from a brown stringy mass. She dumped it into the first cement tub and then, after swirling it around, into the second. Then she lifted it again and dropped it into a bucket of water on the floor. Susie stood on tiptoe and leant forward. She peered through the cobwebs and streaks of dust on the inside of the glass. The woman squatted on the floor and put her hands into the water. She seemed to be running her fingers through whatever was in the bucket, pulling it, untwisting it, stretching it. Then she swung it out of the bucket and back up over the tub. It hung, dripping, from her arm, a long skein of tan-coloured wool.

Susie stared at the brown water running down the Blue Lady's arm and onto the floor. She saw the bags of leaves and grasses that hung from nails on the wall. The steam from the copper filled the room. The woman wiped the sweat from her face with her free arm. She slipped the wool onto the long stick and turned towards the door.

She came out of the side door and around into the yard. She stretched up and balanced the pole holding the wool across the clothesline. Then she ran her hands down the length of the skein, straightening and separating the strands.

*Don't look. Don't find me.*

Susie pushed back, harder into the corner of the laundry and the fence.

The woman gave the wool a final gentle shake, wiped her wet hands down over her hips and turned around.

Eyes meet. The woman steps back, mouth open.

Susie runs. Across the yard to the corner with the toilet. Up onto the fence. Mad scramble. Skin off the knees. Blood. Tunic torn. Scratches. Balance on the top for a second.

'Stop. It's all right. Don't go.' The voice is warm.

But Susie is already over, falling hard on her hands and knees, grabbing her bag from the foot of the tree, running.

# Chapter 7

Susie turned the key and quietly opened the door. She waited a moment but there was no voice from the kitchen, no noise upstairs.

She slid her bag across the dining room floor and went out to the bathroom. The sun had brought her dark freckles out even more. She splashed cold water on her face and looked down at her clothes. Her tunic was stained and torn and there was blood on her socks and shoes from the scratches on her legs. She took her tunic off and pushed it to the bottom of the dirty clothes basket, under the T-shirts and socks from the day before. She pulled on the shorts that had been on top of the pile and washed her hands.

Back in the kitchen she poured herself a long glass of cold water and sat on the step that led to the dining room. *Why run? Why? She wouldn't have done anything.*

She turned the glass in her hands.

*You don't know how some people can be.*

She kicked her shoes off, then peeled off her socks and let them fall to the floor. Blood and dirt mixed together. She started to push the socks down inside the green garbage bag that leant against the kitchen door. It smelt of wet chicken skin and old potato peelings. Her fingers brushed a crumpled envelope. She pulled it out and smoothed it against her leg. It was the airmail envelope from her father.

*Why did he write?*

*No real reason. He just wanted to.*

A tiny piece of torn paper was stuck to it by a splash of gravy.

A letter at Christmas and sometimes a present for Susie. Three story books, in Italian, and when she was nine, a doll, even though she stopped playing with dolls when she was seven.

The front door opened. Susie screwed the envelope and the paper up and pushed them down into the pocket of her shorts. She stood up and when her mother came down the hall, she was standing at the bench drawer, taking out the knives and forks to set the table.

'Hi,' she said, and turned round.

Her mother dropped her shopping bags on the kitchen table. She kicked her sandals off and went to the fridge. 'Boy, it's hot out there.' She poured a drink of juice and sat on the kitchen stool, flapping her skirt to cool her legs. 'Did you have a good day?'

Susie nodded. 'Not bad.'

'I stopped to do the shopping on the way home.' Her mother paused for a moment. 'I ran into Nina. I was going to invite her back for tea, but I decided not to.' She grinned.

Susie shrugged. 'I won't yell at her, next time.'

'I didn't know that.' Her mother hesitated as if to say more, then thought better of it and went across to the bench. 'I came past Kim's old place. There was a pile of blinds and junk out the front. I wonder if she's going to renovate?'

'Wreck it, you mean.'

'Oh, Suse. I'll make some salad.'

Susie took the cutlery into the dining room and then came back to the kitchen for the plates. She bent over to reach into the back of the cupboard.

'Susie?'

Susie didn't move. Her mother was staring at the backs of her legs, at the streaks of blood.

Susie straightened up and put the plates on the bench top.

'What on earth have you done to yourself?'

'A couple of scratches.'

'Scratches! What happened?'

'I was climbing this tree and I slipped and scratched myself getting down.'

'That tree at the back of Sonya's?'

'I didn't go to Sonya's.

'Where did you go then?'

'I was just mucking around. In the park and that.'

'Susie O'Neil, you would be the most infuriating person, sometimes. Can you give a straight answer to a straight question? Where did you get covered in scratches this afternoon?'

Susie turned to face her mother. She took a deep breath. 'I was climbing the tree at the back of Kim's place. I just wanted to see it all again. And that woman, the one I told you about, was in the backyard. She was . . . She was just hanging stuff on the line . . .'

Her mother leant forward.

'Susie.' Her voice was quiet and deliberate. 'Do you mean to tell me you were spying on someone? You climbed that tree so you could look in on someone else's yard?'

'It's only Kim's place.'

'Kim doesn't live there any more.'

'Well, the woman didn't know I was there.'

'That's not the point.' Her mother's voice was tired.

'How would you like it if someone sat up a tree and spied on you all the time?'

'David does.'

'David's different. You know him.' Her mother leant back against the sink. She folded her arms. 'I just don't know what to say. We talked about it this morning. I told you not to go near the cemetery.'

'That wasn't the cemetery.'

'Don't be a smart-alec, Susie. I don't have to spell everything out for you. You know that I include Kim's house in that. This lady is a poor old woman. She's probably got some funny ways and I don't want you hanging around her. O.K.? It's just spying on her.'

'I was not spying.'

'Well, what would you call it?'

Susie turned away. 'It wasn't like that.'

There was a pause for a moment. She felt her mother's hand on her shoulder. Her voice was gentle. 'Look, Suse. I know it's hard for you with Kim gone.'

'Don't call me that.' Susie pulled away. 'I don't care that Kim's gone. That's not the problem.'

'Well, what is?'

Susie stood gripping the kitchen counter, staring at the blue and white pattern on the plates. 'I don't know. It's not fair.'

'What's not fair?'

'I don't know. Everything.'

Her mother began to wash the lettuce. She pulled the leaves from around the heart and plunged them into a sink of cold water. Then she tore them into pieces and dropped them into the metal colander. 'I don't want to hear any more about it,' she said. She tipped the lettuce into a bowl and began to slice tomatoes, quickly. 'And I definitely do not want you going near Kim's house or the cemetery

53

again.' The red juice and the seeds spilled over the breadboard. 'If you want to be a help, you can finish setting the table.'

Susie grabbed the plates and went up into the dining room. 'Who wants to help?' she muttered.

'What was that?'

'Nothing.'

After tea, Susie sat at her table upstairs and looked at her project book. It was long and thin with a spiral back and she had covered it with blue paper. She pushed it aside and knelt down and took the shoebox out from under the bed. The drawing, the one of just her, was on the top. She spread it on the desk, smoothing out the creases. She felt under the desk for some Blu-Tack. There was always a small, soft ball stuck like chewing gum on the wood near her right knee. She went over to the mirror and put the drawing up level with her face. She looked from one to the other. She tilted her head at the same angle as the drawing, dropping her jaw slightly. She tried to smooth down the sticking-out piece of hair and she licked her finger and wet her eyebrows at the point above her nose where they stood straight up. It was all exact. Susie shivered. She tried to turn her eyes away in the manner of the drawing, to capture the expression, but each time she tried, she could no longer see herself.

'Su-se, you doing your homework?'

'Yes.'

She sat down at the desk and pulled the project in front of her. The instruction sheet was stuck on the inside of the cover.

*You and your classmates have decided to establish a new society, Utopia, in an isolated area. There is a good supply of water and*

54

*other natural resources. You have built*
*accommodation and now it is time for*
*everyone to begin working in this new*
*community. Decide which jobs are*
*important and why. Then allocate those jobs*
*to members of the class.*

She started to colour the letters for Utopia. They took up the centre of the title page, thick capitals with careful shadows. Behind the heading she had drawn her new city, some tall towers, houses on a hillside and, on the edge of the buildings, a huge tent with flags on top. Carefully drawn characters, outlined in black and coloured with magic marker made a border for the page.

*Kim. Change Kim . . .*

*In our new city we want everyone to be happy so we have a town circus. Kim and I will run the circus. She will be the ringmaster and I will paint the scenery and the posters to advertise each show. We are both acrobats too and the stars of the show. Tanya and Cheryl are the trapeze artists. Johnno is the funniest person in the class so he can be the clown.*

*David and Peter both like eating a lot so they can be the bakers and make bread and cakes and lollies for us every day.*

*No one wants to be the garbageman so a robot does that . . .*

Susie took a bottle of Liquid Paper from the window sill and carefully blotted out 'Kim'. She sat for a moment twisting a pencil between the fingers of her right hand. *Kim. Sonya? Michelle? . . .*

55

She leant back on her chair.

*Acrobats. Why not artists?* She picked up a pencil and a notebook from the back of the desk. She sketched quickly, broad sweeping strokes, filling the page with cartoon faces. She drew girls. Girls with short, spiked hair, bushy curly hair, long-haired girls with huge eyes and full pouting lips. When there was no more room on the page she ripped it from the book, screwed it tightly into a hard ball and tossed it into a far corner of the room.

She fell back onto her chair and pushed her hands into the pockets of her shorts. The crumpled envelope. It was still there. She smoothed it on her knee and read her mother's name: Signora Martha O'Neil, and their address. She turned it over. Scribbled on the back, half-smudged was: 'Mitt. Sig. V. Simpson'.

The torn piece of paper was still stuck against the envelope. She pushed it gently with her fingernail. It fell away and drifted to the floor. She bent down and picked it up.

*What if it's in Italian? If I can't read it?*

*Don't be stupid. He grew up in Australia. He spoke English with Mum.*

. . . . . . . . . *look forward to seeing you . . . . for
the first time, knowing Susannah . . . .*
                                *Victor.*


Victor. Her father. *Look forward to seeing you.* He must be coming. For the first time. But he almost never wrote. Never came. Wanted nothing to do with them.

Susie sat on the floor, hugging her knees. She chewed her bottom lip and stared at the scrap of paper.

*Why didn't she tell me? He is my father.*

56

Kim's dad lived with them.

Michelle's dad lived on the other side of the Harbour Bridge.

'My father,' Susie had said to them one recess under the jacaranda tree, 'lives on the other side of the world.'

At the school sports carnival last year Kim's dad took the morning off work and won the fathers' race. He was puffing and blowing but he laughed and took them to McDonald's for tea.

'Why,' she said to Mum, 'why doesn't he live with us?' They sat on the floor in the loungeroom and stretched their cold hands out to the warm metal columns of the heater.

Her mother brushed her hair. It was long that winter and fell forward over her shoulders. 'These things happen,' she said.

'Why?' Susie said again.

'Because he was happy in Milan and I wasn't. Because he had a job and friends and I didn't. I was stuck in a tiny flat and I was lonely and I wanted to come home and I missed my mother. And you were born and I really think that he wasn't ready to settle down . . .'

'You mean he didn't want me.'

'That's not what I said.'

'But that's what you meant.'

Susie's mother wrapped her arms around her daughter's shoulders and hugged her. 'Two overgrown kids travelling the world is not a good start for a marriage, Suse. It could never have worked.'

'I hate him.' Susie buried her face in the thick wool of her mother's jumper.

'No, you don't.' She gave Susie the photos then. Two snapshots taken in the mountains, in the snow. There is ice on the curly black hair, ice on the moustache. He has laughing black eyes and a dimple. In one hand he has a snowball and he is coming towards the camera as if he is going to toss it in the face of the photographer.

'You have these, Suse. One day you'll feel differently. You might want to know him. I'll tell you more then.'

But Susie never asked and she never said.

*Look forward to knowing Susannah . . .*

Susie clenched her fists and pressed them into the rug. She looked across at the drawing stuck against the mirror, the photo of her father on the dressing table, the snaps of Kim.

A hot breeze blew in the window.

*Just pictures.*

She dropped her face to her knees, pressing down till her eyes hurt and balls of light bounced in the darkness behind her lids.

# Chapter 8

'Let's start then, shall we?' Mr Marsden smiled brightly at the group around the corner table. His red forehead sweated.

'You first, David. Tell us your jobs and the people you've allocated to them.' He frowned at someone whispering in the next group and moved to a position beside the window where he could watch the whole class.

David screwed up his face and then opened his project book and pushed it forward so they could all see.

*What's he made me? Gardener on the Council like his mum? Work in the hospital like mine?*

Susie looked around the group. Michelle and Mai, Carlos, Jason and David. Used to be Kim, too. A group for all their work. They sat in the corner by the heater under the seven papier-mâché fish, hanging from the ceiling, left over from Education Week. She'd made the one with turquoise gills with David.

'. . . and I think the best job in the world is ski instructor so that's what I'm going to be.'

'But you can't ski.'

'Doesn't matter. It's imagination.'

'And anyway. There's no snow.'

'There is in my town.'

'Go on, David,' said Mr Marsden. He went over to the

next table, ducking to miss a fish tail.

David turned the page. 'Carlos can be the doctor and Jason can be the teacher 'cause they're both brainy and Alessandro can be the builder because he's best at woodwork.' He grinned and looked around the table.

'What about us?' said Susie. 'You haven't said any girls yet.' She looked to Michelle and Mai. They nodded. 'Sexist.'

'Hang on a sec. I'm getting there.' He studied the page and read carefully. 'Most of the girls will stay home with the children. Some will work. Susie and Michelle will sweep the streets and collect the garbage.'

'Hey! That's not fair. I let you be a baker and a shopkeeper and eat lollies.' Susie yelled across the table at David.

'I can do what I like,' David hissed back at her. 'I'm the boss of my town. You girls think you're so smart. You're stuck-up, too good to talk to us. Well, you can do the lousy jobs.' He stood up. The whole class was watching. Chairs scraped back as groups turned around.

'Then I'm going to change mine so you clean the toilets . . .'

'Do what you like! I don't care.' David fell back into his chair.

Someone in the group by the door started cheering. 'Go to it, Davo.'

Susie thumped the table and leapt to her feet.

'Quiet! Susie! David! What on earth is going on?' Mr Marsden was back at his desk. 'Come here at once.' They came and stood before him, not looking at each other. The rest of the class was still.

'Well? I'm waiting for an explanation.'

Silence.

'I want to know what that was all about.'

Susie could see, above and behind him, on the board the beginning of the spelling list for the week, nouns in red chalk, verbs in green.

| belief | believe |
| relief | relieve |

'Nothing,' said Susie.

'Nothing, sir,' said David.

'NOTHING!' roared Mr Marsden. 'You two yell and scream at each other, bang the desk in front of the whole class, and you have the hide, no the effrontery, to say, "Nothing".' He slapped his open hand down on a pile of books. His eyes bulged and the veins in the side of his nose grew redder. Susie counted to ten, slowly. He always took that long. He became quiet. The whole room was still as he leant forward and smiled, his top lip curling back into his moustache. 'Perhaps at lunchtime you will have changed your minds a little. I'll speak to you then. Sit down.'

Tracey and Sonya in the group near the door giggled.

'And I'll have no noise from the rest of you or you can join them.'

At lunchtime he sent them to pick up papers.

'Fifty each,' he said and pointed them in opposite directions. Susie went towards the Infants' playground

*It's not fair. I didn't start it.*

She picked up two sandwich wrappers and an empty chip packet.

*Rip them up. Tear them into tiny bits. Make fifty pieces easily and take them to him. Dump them on his desk. Here's your fifty papers. Stick them in the bin yourself.*

She turned at the climbing bars and headed for the bubblers. She glanced across at the verandah. Mr Marsden was watching her. He stood on the top step, arms folded, rocking gently, backwards and forwards.

David was moving quickly around the back fence, pulling at the papers caught in the wire.

*Stuck-up, are we? Just because they weren't invited to the party.*

*Serves them right. They're so childish.*

Michelle waved from her spot under the jacaranda tree. The others had their heads down, looking at something Sonya held in her hand.

*More party stuff. They can keep it.*

Her fist clenched.

*I'll make Utopia a whole city just for me and Kim. No boys. No Blue Lady. No Mum. No other kids. We'll do just what we want all the time.*

She'd lost count of the number of papers she had and two little boys were staring at her. She poked her tongue out and they ran away.


After school she stood at the gate.

'You going up the street?' Michelle came towards her, her bag dragging on the ground. 'Mum says I can try those jeans on today.'

'No. Got something else to do.'

Michelle didn't move. 'We decided this thing today. While you were picking up papers.'

'Oh?'

'Yeah. Because Lisa reckons we're all too young to come to her party, we're all going to show her. We all have to dye our hair, really bright colours. Pink and green and orange. Sonya and Tanya reckon you can get this stuff at the chemist. It just washes out all right.'

'And is everyone going to do it?'

'Yeah. You have to too.'

'Yeah, maybe.'

'Come on, Susie. Don't wreck it.' Michelle leant against the fence.

Kids raced past.

'See ya.'

'Bye.'

Michelle looked closely at Susie. 'Do you still reckon that you're not going to do it? Play the game, I mean.'

Susie nodded. 'You didn't tell?'

Michelle shook her head. 'What are you going to do?'

'It's a secret. I can't tell anyone.' She swung her bag over her shoulder. 'I've got to go now. See you.'

'See you.'

They walked off in opposite directions. Susie never went this way. Down to the roundabout, past the hospital, through the car park and across the oval.

*Plan 1. Get sick. Get some terrible, horrible disease and not go to the party.*

*Mum would never believe it.*

*Plan 2. Go to the party. Lead a revolt against the game. Say No!*

*Tanya would never agree. Nor would Sonya. Michelle might.*

*Plan 3. Go to the party. Then get sick. Throw up and have to go home.*

*Plan 4. Escape!*

She crossed the road, past the statue out the front of the hospital for mothers and babies. Once, in first class, she'd said she was born there and Mum had said no, she wasn't, she was born in Italy.

A car pulled up just ahead of her and a man and a little girl got out.

'I've got a new baby,' the girl said to Susie.

'Have you?'

'And a new dolly and three new books.'

The man grinned at Susie. 'We had another girl this morning. I'm going to have a house full of women.' He had a huge bunch of flowers and he had the doll tucked under one arm. He took the little girl by the hand. 'Say bye-bye.'

She didn't, but let go and raced up to the steps that led to the heavy glass doors.

*A house full of women. Mum. Me. Did my Dad bring flowers? When I was born, did he see me? What did he think? Why wasn't he ready? Why didn't he want me?*

She started to run. A slight breeze cooled her face and her tunic flapped around her legs. Across the road, a man high up on scaffolding whistled and waved. She kept running towards the oval at the bottom of the hill.

Susie climbed the mound to the small band rotunda that overlooked the playing area. She dropped down onto the dry grass that surrounded it, leant back against her schoolbag and shielded her eyes from the afternoon sun.

Two straight rows of boys faced each other on either side of the cricket pitch. Their coach, in tiny shorts and a green T-shirt, punched his fist into the palm of his hand. His voice boomed over the oval, the tired-looking rose garden, the children's playground and the bowling green.

'We're going to throw, throw, throw. You're going to get so tired that you're going to want to lie down on the grass and at that point we're going to run and jog until you lot are the fittest, the fastest, the best team in the competition.'

He tossed cricket balls onto the pitch.

Susie watched the balls flying through the air. From one row to the other. Back again. She lay back and looked at the sky.

'Throw, throw, throw. Step back. Make that gap wider.'

The sun burned her bare legs. She opened her schoolbag and took out an exercise book and a pencil. She started to draw, doodling in wide sweeping strokes. They started as the full flight sails of ships or giant waves but then grew smaller and smaller, crossing back on each other till the page was a mass of lines. Down the edge of the page she drew heads; the back view with long hair caught in a loose bun at the neck.

*She draws me. I'll draw her.*

She took a fresh page and tried to draw the Blue Lady's face. Broad forehead, wide cheekbones, surrounding mass of hair. That was the easy part. She closed her eyes and tried to imagine the rest. *Jess.* She said the name softly. *What shape was the nose? How did the eyes look? How many wrinkles? How to get that look that saw through you? Jess.*

She drew and crossed out and tried to draw again.

The swing in the playground squeaked.

'Wheee!'

'Watch out!'

Laughing. Loud voices laughing.

Susie looked up. Three older kids were leapfrogging across the grass. They'd come from the swings and the slippery dip. Up and over each other. Then down, hands on knees, head bent. Up and over. The girl leaping had a tight black skirt on. She got stuck on her friend's back. He took off, piggybacking her around the roses. She kept laughing, her head thrown back, her spiky orange hair unmoving in the wind. The second boy, collapsed on the grass, cheered them on.

Susie watched as all three rolled under the trees and still laughing and yelling to each other ran arm-in-arm around the oval to the gate behind the bowling club.

Again the harsh voice came.

65

'Stop looking at those weirdos. Come on. Throw!'

Susie sat up. She ran her fingers through her short hair, so it stood straight up from her head. It fell back, and she picked up her bag and headed for the gate.

She waited for her mother on the seat below the cemetery wall. They waved to each other and met in the middle of the park where the two paths crossed.

'Did you have a good day?' said Mum.

'All right,' said Susie. 'Did you?'

'Same old stuff.'

'You know what, Mum? Bloody old Marsden made me pick up papers today. Just because I yelled at David because he made me a garbage man.'

'Who?'

'*Mr* Marsden.'

'That's better. A garbage man?'

'You know. The project.'

'Oh, the project. How did that go? Did Mr Marsden tell you how good the drawings were?'

'I just told you. I had to pick up papers. And he didn't even look at the drawings. We didn't finish. I'm not even going to get to talk about mine till after next week.'

'Well, I'm sure he will . . . And you and David will be friends again.' She rested her hand on Susie's shoulder. 'God, I'm tired.'

'We will not,' said Susie. 'He's a childish creep and I hate him.'

They crossed the road.

'I ran into Michelle's mother at lunchtime,' Susie's mother said. 'She told me she was buying some new clothes for Sonya's party. I thought we might get something nice for you too.'

# Chapter 9

'You think I'm being a bit hard on her, don't you?'

The voice was low. Susie crept down the first three stairs.

'Come on, Nina. What can I do? I've always been strict about strangers. She knows what she's been doing is wrong.'

Pause.

'What?'

Susie leant against the banister. The phone was under the stairs and she could see her mother's hair, uncombed.

'Yeah. I did ask Betty next door. She told me quite a story about a broken heart . . . She says the woman's lived around here for years and is quite harmless.'

There was a long pause. Susie studied the poster of mammals on the opposite wall. It was stuck over the spot where the water leak made the paint peel. Somewhere under the ringtail possum, the water was working away. The poster would fall down again before New Year.

'O.K. I'll try that. I won't mention it to her for a whole day. I'm taking her shopping . . . Oh, and you know that letter from Victor . . .'

The voice trailed off. Susie heard her mother moving with the phone into the front room. She went back upstairs and bounced on the bed.

She tossed a pillow at the poster of Madonna, fell onto her back and then rolled over onto the floor.

'Susie? Is that you getting up?'

'In a minute.'

'C'mon.' The phone clicked. 'We've got things to do.'

They came up the steps and out of St James Station. Susie's mother looked across at the church. 'So long since I've been into town,' she said, 'I can't even pick the right exit any more.'

They walked across the park to Elizabeth Street. Spray from the fountain blew onto their hot arms and legs. Susie skipped sideways, turning her face to the water and spreading her arms wide. 'It's great,' she yelled as drops of water settled in her hair, on her clothes and her bare skin. 'I'm hot, Mum. Can I have an icecream?'

'Later.' Her mother walked quickly to the edge of the footpath.

'C'mon. The lights are green.'

Susie ran to catch up.

'We'll go to Centrepoint,' her mother said. 'There's lots of places there.'

They elbowed their way around crowds of people, past the newspaper-sellers and the man with buckets of red and white carnations. They took the escalator to the basement level. Disco music blared from three different boutiques. A group of big kids, elbows linked, pushed their way through the crowd. Susie moved closer to her mother.

SUSSAN. KATIE'S. RAGGED EDGES. NEW THREADS.

'What about this one?' Susie's mother pointed to a sign, FANTASY, flashing in green neon. Susie took a step towards the door, hesitated and looked in the window instead. Models, their hair in different shades of pink, orange and purple lay on the floor or draped themselves across huge silver boxes. They were all tall and slim with long, elegant lashes and fingernails.

'Come on, Suse.' Her mother, her hands pushed down into the pockets of her jeans, strolled into the shop and straight up to the first rack of dresses.

SPECIALS . . . NOTHING OVER $20.

'What about this lot?' She flicked the coathangers along the rail, pulled one out and called across to Susie. 'Do you like this?'

'Sshh,' said Susie. She glanced sideways and came over to the rack. 'Yuk. It's daggy.' She stuffed the dress back into the middle of the rack.

'D'you want any help?' A salesgirl moved towards them. Her huge black T-shirt was belted at the waist by a broad silver band. She wore skinny black tights and she danced to the music that poured from the speaker sets around the door. She moved her fingers with their black nail polish, and jerked her head so that the long silver earrings jangled.

'No, thanks. We're just looking,' said Susie's mother.

Susie turned to look at the trousers hanging in front of the window. White ones, pale green and blue ones. Prints of flowers, jungles, faces. Tight ones, jeans, loose-flowing billowy ones. Michelle had chosen jeans. What about Tanya? Sonya? She pulled some out to check the size, the style around the waist, the width of the leg.

'Seen something you like?'

Susie pulled a face. 'They're all revolting.'

Her skin, in the green light, looked sick and the T-shirt she'd put on that morning, handpainted six months before in craft, was tight and made her feel eight years old.

'Come on, Susie. They can't all be.' Her mother put her head on one side to admire white cotton pants, printed with blue and yellow palm trees. 'What are all the others wearing? Do you know?'

Susie shook her head. 'I'm always too busy picking up papers to talk to my friends.'

'Be fair,' said her mother. 'That was only once.'

*Once. A million times. It didn't matter. No one told her. Did they want her to come? A daggy party, anyway.*

Susie watched the salesgirl leaning up against the back wall, talking to someone in the changing room, laughing.

She pulled a pair of black trousers from the rack. 'These,' she said. 'I'll try these.'

'Are you sure you want black?'

'Michelle's mother said she can have black.'

Her mother held them up, turned them round and then looked at the price tag. 'Hey, you'll do no such thing. Look at how much they are.'

Susie ran out of the shop. Her mother followed her, almost the length of the arcade. She caught up with her at the foot of the escalator, put a hand on her shoulder and spun her round.

'Don't, Mum. You're embarrassing me.'

'I'll do more than embarrass you. Don't you dare go off in a huff, young lady. Look at me while I'm speaking to you. You know our financial situation, Susie. I wouldn't pay that much for clothes and you're not going to, either.'

'You said I could have what I wanted.'

'I did not say you could have a blank cheque.'

'Well, just forget it. I don't want to go to that stupid bloody party anyway. I hate Sonya and I've got nothing to wear.' Susie tried to turn away. She folded her arms and looked down at the floor. There were thousands of tiny tiles all different shapes and colours, blues, green and gold, fitted together. Her mother tucked her arm under Susie's and stepped onto the escalator.

'Oh, no, you don't. We are not going home till we find you something.'

Susie caught sight of their reflections in the chrome sides of the escalator. Her shoulders were hunched, her head down. Her mother stood, shoulders back, staring straight ahead. Her long white T-shirt was tied in a knot on her hip. Susie dug her fingernails into her sides. She stepped off the escalator and followed her mother across the skywalk to the big department store.

They stopped under the Information sign. A woman in a black dress came up to them. 'Can I help you, madam?' she said.

'We're looking for clothes.'

'For madam or for your little girl?'

'For my daughter. I think the Teen Scene section is what we want.'

They walked through an arch and down some steps.

'Little girl,' Susie sniffed.

'She didn't mean to be like that.'

'Well, why did she say it?'

'Stop worrying, Susie, and think about what you want.'

'Looking for something special, are we?' This saleswoman was old enough to be Susie's grandmother. She wore her hair in a bun, each strand pulled tight. She had rings on three fingers of her left hand and she rubbed her hands together as she talked. The sweat ran down the inside of Susie's jeans.

'Trousers, I think. Size ten. A bit dressy but not too dear.' Her mother grinned at Susie. 'That's right, isn't it?'

They followed the woman across to the racks in an alcove in the apricot-coloured wall.

'You'll find something here,' she said. 'All the young ones are buying these styles. See the overdyeing.' She picked up the leg of a pair of purple trousers and indicated the green thread coming through. 'Or maybe you'd prefer navy and pink?'

'We'll try some on.' Susie's mother nodded to the woman and she left.

Purple with green stitching.

Navy with pink.

Black with yellow.

Bottle green with gold.

Susie's mother sat on the chair outside while Susie tried them on.

*Don't come in till I've got them on. Don't leave the curtain like that, someone might see.*

'Yuk. They look awful.'

'No, they don't. They're just a bit long.' Her mother knelt on the carpet and tucked the bottom of the legs up. 'And when you put a different shirt on and with your hair combed . . .'

'I'll gel it,' said Susie. She pulled it through her fingers till it stood straight up. Her mother raised her eyebrows and tightened her lips. She gathered up the pile of jeans on the floor and went out. She put her head back around the curtain.

'Which colour was it? The green?'

'No,' said Susie. 'The black.'

They sat at a round white table in the open space between two rows of shops. Light poured in from the glass ceiling. Susie sucked noisily on a double milkshake with icecream and strawberry sauce.

'Enjoy it,' said her mother as she sipped her coffee. 'You'll be getting pimples soon.'

Susie took the straw out of the glass and licked the froth that hung from it. Her feet rested on the bag that held the new jeans.

'Mum,' she said, 'why do you reckon Kim hasn't

72

written? She must know I want her to.'

'She will.' Her mother finished her coffee and leant on her elbows on the table. 'She's sure to be just settling in. She'll write.' She grinned across the table at Susie, her skin wrinkling around eyes that were the same warm blue-green as the tiles.

*Tell her about the drawings . . . About wanting to see more . . . Wanting to ask the Blue Lady . . . About what's going to happen at the party . . .*

'You might find that these holidays you have loads of parties and things to do with the other kids and you don't have too much time to even think about Kim.'

Susie looked away. Two girls, a few years older than her, came out of the record shop opposite and went up to the counter to get drinks.

'Look,' her mother said. 'They've got trousers on just like you bought, only blue.'

They had their hair cut straight across at the back. The bits above each ear were trimmed very short and the top stood straight up.

'If you had your hair like that,' said her mother, 'you'd look about fifteen. Make me feel really old.'

Susie grinned. 'They reckon life begins at forty. You're not even born yet.'

'Being in town makes me feel about a hundred. Come on.' Her mother stood up. 'I've had enough for one day. Let's go home and go for a swim.'

# Chapter 10

*SUSIE,*
*Don't cha love this postcard of the band?*
*Unreal . . . . . . . . . .*
*Saw a concert with them on Sat. night. Me, Sharon,*
*Bradley and his friend Mark.*
*I touched someone who touched* Brian Mannix!!!
*I got 3 posters and 2 T-shirts and a record.*
*Luv,*
*Kim*
*P.S. Write to Aunty Joy's:*
    *26 Gipps St,*
    *Carlton.*
    *Vic.*
*(I don't know the postcode.)*


Susie threw the card on the kitchen bench.

'What a dog, Mum. She didn't say she missed me or anything.'

'Su-se.'

'Don't call me that, Mum.'

'Well, don't you speak like that. She probably thought you'd like the card. She'll write you a longer letter later.'

Susie picked the card up, turned it over and glanced at the band.

'Anyway, she knows I hate their music. She can't have forgotten that.'

She read the message again and again. Then she pinned it on the noticeboard over the cupboard, the band's picture to the wall.

'Well, I'm not going to answer it.'

But she did.

> *Same old place.*
> *Second last Tuesday of*
> *school.*

*Dear Kim,*

*At last. About time. i thought you were never going to write. i've got lots and lots of stuff to tell you. i wish you were right here and i could just talk. Are you coming up at Christmas like you said you might? i don't know where to start.*

*School—Yuk. Boring boring boring. i had a big fight with David over the projects and Marsden chucked a you-know-what and made us pick up papers and i hate them both. i didn't get to talk about mine which was good 'cause i haven't finished changing it yet—all the bits with you in it i mean.*

*So i missed out on all the plans for THE PARTY. Sonya's party, well, Lisa's actually. All the stuck-ups from high school will be there and boys. We have to play this game where we have to kiss them and i got the dog turd. That's not his real name. i can't remember it and i don't know what he looks like but he must be daggy or he would've been grabbed by*

75

Lisa. i'm not going to do it. i'm not a leso or anything but i'm not going to do it just because Lisa Mitchell wants it. Tanya's got Nick of course and remember Brett—the one you used to talk about—well Sonya kept him for herself.

The craziest thing of all since you left is the Blue Lady. She did move into your house. Old bag. i keep trying to look in to see if she's changed stuff. i can nearly see into your old room when i go up the tree near the gate and sometimes i go round the back and up the tree over the lane. i still call it your place. i watch her draw and i see her doing other stuff as well. Remember how she used to always get all the grass and stuff from the cemetery— well now i know what she does with it. She dyes. She gets all this wool and she dyes it—mainly browny colours but she also does greeny, yellowy colours too.

i've seen her a couple of times. The first day i got over the fence into your backyard and she saw me. Boy did i run!!!! i was over that fence so fast. Now i'm more careful. i just stay put on a branch where she can't see me. It's great up there. You can see everything (even when that old bloke down the road goes to the loo in his pyjamas and his dog sits at the door and waits till he's finished!).

She does tons of wool. She could make a million jumpers out of it. She's pretty weird. Pete Watson's mum told my mum this story about how years ago she was going to marry this bloke and he dropped her on the day of the wedding. Could you believe it!!! How embarrassing!!!! She never got over it and went a bit funny in the head and cleared out for years and years.

How is everyone? How's Melbourne? Revolting, i hope. Are you coming back for Christmas? Whoops!! i've

*asked you that already. Write me a long, long, long
letter and tell me about everything!!!!!!!!*
     *Write. Write. Write. Write. Write. Write. Write.*
          *Love Soosie*

*P.S. Sonya's as bad as ever. Secrets. Secrets. Secrets.*
*P.P.S. My father has written and i think he's coming
to see us. i wonder what he's like. What will i say to
him???????????*
*P.P.P.S. i am not kissing that turd. i know you'd
really like this party and Lisa'd give you a real
spunk. But i'm going to get really sick and just have
to come home.*
*S.*

Susie left the letter on her desk and went downstairs and
out into the yard. She sat on the steps. It was seven o'clock
but the sun had only just dropped over the houses at the
back. A light breeze from the south cooled her cheeks.

*Why not tell Kim about the drawings? Tell her about
wanting to see more of what the woman did.*

*But Kim said, 'You'll probably go crazy like her . . .'*

Susie leant forward, her head on her knees. The wind
rustled the leaves of the apricot tree. She looked up.
David's face appeared through the branches. She turned
away.

'How come you aren't up in the cemetery?' David leant
forward and jerked the branch between his legs so it
bounced up and down on the fence. 'You're weird, Susie
O'Neil.'

'Go away. Go on. Clear off.'

' 's a free country. You can't make me.'

Susie jumped up and ran around the side of the house. 'Wanna bet?' She turned the tap on, picked up the hose and dragged it back towards the fence.

David parted the leaves to see what she was doing. 'No!' he yelled. 'No. I didn't mean it.'

'You've been spying on me.' Susie advanced, hose forward.

David backed along the branch. 'Don't,' he yelled. 'Don't.'

The water hit him as he reached the point where the branch met the trunk. His voice was lost in the sounds of splashing water, rustling leaves and the high-pitched laugh of Susie dancing around the yard, the hose waving above her.

Susie went back inside. Her mother was talking on the telephone. She covered the mouthpiece of the receiver and waved her hand towards the table.

'Can you pop up to Maria's? Get me some milk and bread. The money's there.'

'Yes. Yes. I know,' she said to whoever was on the other end of the phone. She arched her brows and mouthed the words to Susie, 'Nina's coming over for tea. In about half an hour.'

The street outside was deserted. Susie smelt stew coming from the Watsons' open front door. From the next house, the blueish light of the television flickered at the end of the hallway.

She crossed the road and ran down the lane, heading for the cemetery. *Check the postbox.* She hadn't been there for days. She could do that and go to Maria's and still be back well before Nina arrived. She ran round the yapping dogs that were on their way home from the park.

The gates were still open. Two more dogs were sniffing

around the roots of the tree. Their owners leant against the front fence, talking. Susie went straight to the gravestone and then a bit further. When she turned around, she couldn't see the dogs or their owners through the trees and thick shrubs. Shadows from the elms and the palms fell across the stone. Susie shivered. She bent quickly and pressed herself against the boat prow. A piece of paper was close to the opening. She grabbed it and brushed her hand around the inside of the hole to check that nothing else was there. Then without waiting to look at what she had found, she ran back along the path.

The men and the dogs were gone. Susie leant back against the big tree's roots, wedging herself into the space large enough to sit, and pulled out the paper. She smoothed it on her knee and bent down close to it in the fading light. It was another pen drawing, this time of a tree. It was drawn as though the artist was level with the first branches. The roots of the tree seemed to thrust up from the soil. They were massive roots, broad and gnarled, and they came up to meet the eye of the viewer. Susie drew in her breath. It was this tree. Her tree. She ran her hand over the rough bark she was sitting on. Her special tree. The thick branches filled the paper. In the middle of the black lines of leaves, was another line. Lead pencil, this time, it showed, peeping out from behind a branch, part of a face. Her face. The rest was hidden by leaves. Susie looked at the house across the road.

*Drawn from the upstairs balcony.*
*She knew.*

Across the road there was a light on in Kim's bedroom. The Blue Lady's room, upstairs at the front. The woman herself came across to the windows, stood for a moment in silhouette, her arms outstretched to the edges of the curtains. Then she drew the heavy material in and stepped back again out of sight.

Susie grew cold staring at the darkened window. She heard the currawongs circling above the church and felt the shadows of the trees and bamboo reaching out over her.

Susie ate in the backyard with Nina and her mother. The smoke from the barbecue drifted above them. Chicken fat spat onto the coals making tiny flames light up the side fence.

'So how's school?' said Nina.

'All right.' Susie sipped her drink.

'Your mum says some old lady has moved into Kim's house.'

Susie didn't look at her. 'She's not that old.'

Her mother went across to the fire and came back carrying the long barbecue fork. A piece of chicken dangled from the end. It dripped fat and sauce on the cement.

'I haven't told you the latest,' she said as she slid onto the bench. 'I got accosted up the street by the lady who lives next door to Kim's old house. She went on and on about how she'd rather have a bunch of students living there than that old girl. Says she's up till all hours, playing music and making a racket. And when she tried to have a conversation with her, nothing.'

Nina took the piece of chicken. She dropped it on her plate and licked her greasy fingers. 'Artistic temperament,' she said. 'Didn't you say she draws?'

Susie's mother nodded. 'I don't know what, though. Have you seen anything, Suse?'

Susie looked at her plate. The picture of the tree was folded and put with the others under her bed. She stabbed her piece of chicken with her fork.

'No,' she said. 'I think it's just the church and stuff like that.'

'Betty, next door, has been talking about her again,'

said Susie's mother. 'She repeated the whole story about how she was dumped by that bloke.' She finished her chicken and reached across the table for some bread. 'She added a few bits too about some other woman she knows telling her that there was a kid involved, when she lived away, overseas they think. No one knows what happened to her. She certainly didn't come back with her mother, as far as they know. She could be dead.' She shuddered. 'That'd be enough to send me round the twist.'

They ate in silence for a while, juicy chicken, baked potatoes and two kinds of salad. They wiped the sweat from their foreheads with the backs of their hands and slapped at the mosquitoes that landed on their bare feet.

Nina stretched back in her chair. 'What are you wearing tomorrow night? Did you get something new?'

Susie nodded. 'Jeans. They're no big deal.'

New overdyed jeans hanging in the cupboard.

*It'll be really dark and you have to kiss him and we have to count . . .*

*. . . I'm going to get really sick and have to come home . . .*

'You'll have a really great time.' Nina grinned across at Susie's mother. 'What about us, eh, Martha? We're not too old to party. We'll show . . .' She stopped suddenly at the raised eyebrows and tight mouth of the other woman. She stood up and started to gather the plates.

Susie looked from one to the other.

'What if I go up to the cakeshop and get something for dessert?' said Nina. 'Want to come?'

'No,' said Susie's mother. 'I'll stay here with Susie. There's something I want to tell her.'

Nina left and Susie looked at her mother, waiting.

'It's about tomorrow night.' Her mother leant forward

81

and picked the last bit of lettuce out of the salad bowl. She ate it then licked her fingers. 'Sonya's mother rang me today.'

*It's off. The party's off.*

'She wants all you girls to stay the night.'

'No way.' Susie shook her head.

'Hang on a minute. Let me finish.'

'I am not staying there.' *Giggling all night. Ten girls in a room. All saying who kissed them and where and how and for how long. They'll ask what it was like and . . .*

'I said, let me finish.' Susie's mother folded her arms and looked directly at her. 'I have been invited to a party myself. I wasn't going to go and then Sonya's mother rang up about sleeping over. I said I'd let her know, but I've had a think about it and,' she shrugged her shoulders. 'Damn it all, Susie. I hardly ever go out. You never get left if you don't want to. Anyway I'm going to go and you're going to stay the night with the other kids and that's that.'

Susie picked at the chicken grease under her fingernails. 'Are you going to stay out all night?'

'No, of course not. Don't be silly.'

'I am not being silly.'

Her mother's voice was tired. 'But I will be home quite late and I don't want Mrs Mitchell having to wait up till I can pick you up.'

'I could come home anyway by myself.'

'And get bashed or worse on the way home. Now you *are* being silly. I don't know what's the matter with you these days, Suse.'

*Don't call me Suse.*

'You used to love staying the night at Kim's place. It'll be just the same.'

'It will not.'

Kim and Susie sleep in their T-shirts, talk and eat under the sheets, play the Walkman that Kim got for Christmas, one set of earphones, talk. Talk about Sonya, Tanya, all the kids, and what it would be like at high school, and boys and bras and periods.

Her mother leant over and took Susie's hand. 'Susie, Kim's gone. You aren't the first person to feel sad that someone's gone and you won't be the last. It takes a while but you'll get over it. And spending time with your friends is the best way.' She grinned and squeezed her hand. 'I'll make some coffee. Nina's sure to bring back something yummy and sticky.'

# Chapter 11

Susie stood in the doorway, looking at her clothes laid out on the bed. On top of the new jeans was a fancy T-shirt of her mother's – the one Nina gave her for Christmas. It was pink and had a woman's face handpainted on it, big bright eyes and a wide, smiling mouth. There were clean knickers and clean socks.

*Like birthday parties in Kindergarten. Don't forget to give her the present and say thank you to her mother and only one chocolate crackle or you'll be sick.*

*Tell me what to do now, Mum.*

On the floor was the overnight bag for her pyjamas and toothbrush.

*You used to love staying the night at Kim's place. It'll be just the same.*

She went across to the window and leant out. A few lights had come on in the city though it wasn't yet fully dark. The lights glowed against the navy blue sky. To her right was the tall, dark church spire. Opposite Kim's. She tried to remember the things in Kim's room . . . Two single beds, an old wardrobe painted white, the cane toybox under the window. There was something else behind the door and posters on the walls. Susie closed her eyes to try and bring back the faces of the bands, the colours . . .

'It's all yours,' called her mother from the bathroom.

Susie gathered up the clothes and went downstairs. Her mother stood in front of the bathroom mirror. She was bending over, rubbing her hair dry. The soft curls of her old perm fell around her face. She grinned and dropped the towel on the edge of the bath. She stepped into a black jumpsuit and pulled it up over her hips, pushing her arms into the sleeves and drawing her breath in as she pulled up the zip.

'Come on, Susie. Get a move on. And wash your hair, too.'

She reached into the cabinet for some make-up. Susie stood in the doorway behind her and watched as she rubbed the thick white cream over her hands and onto her face. The glass was steamed up and her mother had rubbed a clean circle in the middle. Her face filled the space. Outside it, blurred but growing clearer, was Susie's reflection.

Her mother smoothed on some liquid make-up, blending it in with long strokes of her fingers. 'It's Jack's fortieth birthday,' she said. 'You know, that ex-boyfriend of Nina's.' She raised her eyebrows and brushed white powder into the arch. Then pale blue on the lids and mascara, thick on her black lashes. She grinned, in the mirror, at Susie. 'She reckons that he's going to have all this old rock and roll music.' She clicked her fingers and swung her hips. 'Do you wanna dance? Da, da, da.'

She giggled and twirled round. 'I wonder if I still remember how to do it. You know, your father was a fabulous dancer. He could swing you forward and back, bend you over, through his legs, the lot.' She turned back to the mirror. 'All I need is a bit of lippie, as my old mum used to say . . .' She smiled at her reflection and stretched her lips over her teeth. She painted on the red lipstick, pressed her lips together and then stood back, patting her flat stomach.

'Mirror, mirror on the wall, who is the fairest one of all?'

She raised her eyebrows, turned to Susie and held her arms out from her sides.

'Well, what do you think?'

Susie sat on the edge of the bath, her hair wet from the shower. She dried her feet on the thick white towel and pulled on her knickers. She opened the bathroom cabinet and took out the razor her mother used. It had a pink plastic handle but the head was cold steel. She turned it over a couple of times and touched the head carefully. *Which was the sharp bit? How did you use it?* She rubbed a bit of wet soap under her armpit. It caught on the half-dozen pale hairs. She twisted her head to try to see what she was doing then turned to watch in the mirror. Slowly she brought the razor down against her white skin. Done. The hairs and soap were trapped against the blade. She rinsed them under the tap and wiped the soap from her bare arm. She lifted the other one. Down again. The edge of the razor nicked the soft skin and blood spurted.

'Ouch!' She dropped the razor into the basin and pressed a towel to the blood. Bright red against the white cotton. She found iodine in the cabinet and dabbed it on. It stung and spread a rich, yellow stain that filled her armpit and dribbled down the side of her chest.

She covered the cut with a bandaid and tried to wipe the blood off the floor with a washer. She stuffed it and the towel into the dirty clothes basket.

'Are you finished, Susie?'

'Nearly.'

'You can have a bit of my perfume if you like.'

She washed her hands and stood back to look at herself in the mirror. The hairs of her eyebrows stood straight up. She licked her fingers and smoothed them back into a sleek line. She screwed her nose up at the brown freckles that spread across her cheeks and the shaggy hair that flopped over her eyes and stuck out above her ears. She picked up the make-up base that her mother had just used. It was dark, right for suntans. She poured some of it onto her hand and started to rub it over her face. It streaked, almost orange over her pale cheeks. *Yuk!* She rubbed it in hard. That was worse. She splashed water on her cheeks, took a washer and rubbed harder. It started to come off. Her skin glowed red raw. She dropped the washer into the hand basin and let her arms fall to her sides.

*Lisa says we're just a bunch of little kids . . .*

She took up the palate of eye shadows and held the colours in front of her. Green for her eyes? Blue to match the eyes on the front of her T-shirt? She chose the green, dusted some onto the tiny brush and poked with it at her eyelid. She winked, blinked, twisted her face and then held her eye closed with her free hand. It wouldn't go on evenly. Heavy at one end, light at the other. She put on more, then scraped some off with the corner of her towel. Then the mascara. She poked the end of the wand into the corner of her eye. It smarted and watered. *Red like crying.* The bit she had got on came off when she blinked and black lines ran down onto her cheeks.

'What are you doing, Susie? Hurry up.'

Susie took a clean washer and carefully wiped her cheeks and forehead. She looked in the mirror. Her green eyelids sparkled. She grinned and ran her fingers through her hair.

*We all have to dye our hair.*

But when Michelle gave her half a packet of pink hair dye she'd dumped it in the bin outside Maria's shop.

The front of her hair fell forward, the sides stuck out. She stared for a minute, pulling the side bits between her thumb and forefinger, watching them settle. She opened the cabinet again and took out the big jar of white cream that her mother had used. She smeared some on her palm and ran her hand back from forehead to crown. The hair stood up. Straight. She touched the tips of the peaks. Then she bent down, picked up the razor and held it against her head.

*Come back, Mum. Come and stop me. Say we have to leave right now.*

She held a side piece out from her head.

'Susie! I am not going to wait all night. I'm going to get some wine up the street. Just be ready when I get back because I'm leaving then.'

The razor came down. The side piece fell to the floor. Susie watched the mirror closely and moved the razor slowly. She bit her bottom lip. It was too hard to work out which way to move the razor in the mirror. She felt for the bits of hair and then looked in the mirror to check. Bit by bit she shaved the hair back, almost to her skin. Then the other side. Her face seemed thinner, longer. The sides didn't quite match. She took a little more off the left, then the right, then the left again. Her white scalp showed through the bits of brown hair.

*If you had your hair done like that, you'd look about fifteen.*

She dropped the razor into the sink and spread more cream onto her hands. She rubbed both hands over her head. Clumps of hair stuck together and stood up and out. She turned her head from side to side. The face in the mirror grinned then gulped. The pink T-shirt would look ridiculous.

The front gate clicked. Susie glanced at the open jars, the spilt coloured powder, and raced out of the bathroom and upstairs to her room.

She pulled her jeans and shoes on and then held different shirts against her. Pale blue, white, cream with a lace ruffle. Too neat. Too nice. The front door banged.

'I'm upstairs, Mum. Nearly ready.'

She stood in the middle of her room and looked around quickly. She heard the voice from the bottom of the stairs. 'I am going in one minute.'

Madonna glared down from her poster . . . dressed in layers. T-shirt, shirt, dress, jacket, coat.

Susie picked a red T-shirt up off the floor and put it on. Cream from her hair smeared on the cotton and came off on her back. Then she opened the wardrobe. White school shirts. Black-flecked painting shirt. She held it against her. Too hot. She tore at the sleeves. Nothing happened. She grabbed scissors from the desk and hacked at the material below the shoulder. The sleeves came away in jagged cuts. She put the shirt on and tied the bottom of it round her waist.

Her ears were bare. She tried to hold onto the tiny pieces of hair and tug them down, longer. She licked her fingers and slicked her eyebrows again. She spun round.

*Mirror, mirror on the wall . . .*

Hands on hips, head cocked on the side, eyebrows frowning, turn slowly.

*What would they say? Think? Tanya? Sonya? . . . Mum?*

From the back of the door she took the black sleeveless jacket. The op shop one, shared with Kim. The front panels hung low over her knotted shirt. The lining was

89

torn. She stood for a moment in front of the mirror. Her shoulders drooped.

'Susie! For the last time!'

Susie grabbed her overnight bag from the bed, slowly drew her breath in and opened the door.

# Chapter 12

*'Su-sie!'*

Susie stopped on the stairs.

'What on earth . . .!' The keys dropped from her mother's hands. 'You look . . . You look . . .' Her face reddened. She moved forward under the light and it caught the streaks of grey in her hair. 'Ridiculous.'

Silence.

'Stupid hair. It was daggy anyway.' Susie didn't look at her but scratched at the paint on the side of the staircase.

*Send me back to wash it out. Make me.*

'It was fine. It was clean and . . . and soft and pretty.'

'Pretty daggy,' Susie whispered.

'What did you say?' Her mother drew her breath in and spoke slowly.

'Aren't we running late?' said Susie.

*Tell me I can't go.*

'I can't let you go like this.'

Susie looked up. 'It's just the fashion, Mum. All the kids are doing it.' She played with the ends of the black shirt. *They'd better not've chickened out.*

'This house does not operate on the guiding principle of what "all the kids are doing".'

'You just want me to dress like a baby.'

'Don't be so childish.' Her mother bent to pick up her

keys and bag. 'Mrs Mitchell'll have a fit.'

Susie started for the doorway. 'It's none of her business what I look like. Anyway, Sonya's going to do it too.'

They were quiet till they reached the car. Susie's mother started the engine and sat with both hands on the wheel.

'This is the last thing I'm going to say about it, Suse. I don't like it. But you're the one who's got to wear it. You may not like it yourself for much longer – but you're stuck with it till it grows back. Think about it.' She slipped the car into gear and pulled out from the kerb.

The car stopped in front of the Mitchells' house.

'Not here, Mum. Go on a bit.'

Susie's mother said nothing but ran the car forward for a moment.

Susie grabbed her bag and jumped out. 'See you tomorrow.' As the car pulled away she walked back to Sonya's house. She hesitated at the gate, tugging at the short bits of hair above her ears and shifting her weight from one foot to the other.

Then she bent forward, stuffed her bag between the straggly rosebushes and the wooden fence, and walked up the path.

Sonya stood at the end of the darkened hallway. The light from the loungeroom flowed behind her. Her hair colour was unchanged. Susie waited at the door.

*Damn Sonya.*

She drummed her fingers on the frame.

*All talk.*

'G'day, Susie. Gee, you look fantastic. Come in.' Sonya pushed the screen door open and took Susie's arm. 'Mum freaked out and wouldn't let us and Tracey rang up to say her dad got cranky when she did it and now he won't let her come and she was crying down the phone and everything.'

They reached the loungeroom. Susie let her arm fall free.

Sonya waved at the tall thin man watching television. 'You know my dad.' He nodded without turning round. She took Susie's arm again and led her into the kitchen. 'How come your mum let you cut it? Can I touch it?'

Susie cocked her head to the side. 'No problem. I just did it and she couldn't do a thing. You can't stick it back.'

The kitchen was empty.

'There's no one from our class here yet. There's a few of Lisa's friends out the back. Snobs.'

'Where's your mum?'

'Up at the shop.' Sonya went around to the other side of the kitchen table and took some plates off the counter. 'We wanted them to go out but they wouldn't.' She turned and held them out to Susie. 'Peanuts or chips?'

Susie took a handful of chips and went into the sunroom. 'We can go outside if you like,' said Sonya, but they stood for a moment, watching Lisa, two other girls and three boys standing under the clothesline. The orange lights, strung from the back of the house, made Nick Soulos look sick. He wore tight jeans and a shirt unbuttoned to the waist.

'Is Tom What's-'is-name here yet?' whispered Susie.

Sonya shook her head.

'Maybe he's not coming.'

*Don't come.*

'They always come late. That's what Lisa says. Only dags come early.'

'Thanks a lot.'

'Oh, Susie, I didn't mean you.' Sonya dug her in the ribs with her elbow. She took a handful of peanuts. 'Mum and Dad are going to bed early. They've promised. That's when we're going to play the game.'

*Georgie Porgie pudding and pie,*
*Kissed the girls and made them cry.*

*Not me. Not cry.*

'Where's your stuff for tonight Susie?'
*Don't ask.*
'Sonya.' Mrs Mitchell, tall, her heels thudding on the carpet came down the hall.

'There you are. Hello, dear.' She arched an eyebrow. 'Oh! It's Susie. I didn't recognise you.' She pushed a bag of soft drink across the table. 'There's more guests arriving. Go and welcome them.'

Susie followed Sonya back up the hall. Cheryl, Tanya and Michelle were standing on the step. They each held an overnight bag and they stood close together under the front light.

'Come on. Come in,' said Sonya. She led them into the first room off the hall.

'This is my room. Mine and Lisa's. This is my bed.' She bounced back against a tired-looking teddy bear and two Cabbage Patch dolls.

Michelle leant forward and touched Susie's hair. 'Looks great. I did mine green and got it to stand right up but Dad made me wash it out. He reckoned I looked like a slut. I told him we were all doing it but he wouldn't listen.'

Tanya nodded. 'My mum said that too. It was all I could do to paint my fingernails.' She held out her hand with the black polish. 'I brought it with me. Do you want some?'

They sat on the floor and took turns. Tanya applied the polish with a steady hand. When she finished, Susie

94

held her hands in front of her mouth and blew on them. Cracked, chewed nails. But black.

'How come your mum let you do your hair?' said Tanya.

'She didn't,' said Susie. 'In fact,' she looked around the group, 'she said I could come to the party but I couldn't stay the night. I have to leave at ten o'clock.'

*That was easy.*

'What a drag.'

'You mean you have to go home?'

'But we might hardly have started then.'

*Good. Who wanted to start? When the game started. Off. Down the side lane. Pick up the overnight bag. Home.*

Susie shrugged. 'I tried to talk her out of it—but she nearly stopped me coming at all.'

They left the room together, giggling in the darkened hallway.

'Hi, girls.' Nick came out of the kitchen carrying two jugs of punch. He had put some music on the tape recorder and he swayed in time to it. 'Follow me if you want some fun.' He winked over his shoulder as he went down the back steps. He put the jugs down on the table and turned to watch the girls coming towards him. Susie stayed in the doorway with Sonya.

'I reckon he's full of himself.'

'Tanya doesn't think so.'

Tanya stayed outside. Michelle and Cheryl drifted back in. Juice in hand, they came to check their hair, to find a tissue, to drape themselves over the sunroom sofa and talk. Susie explained how she'd done her hair. Michelle told them how she hadn't been able to find her sandals and the whole family had to help look for them. Cheryl started to talk about the group that her sister had gone to see at the Entertainment Centre but the others had never heard of them and went and watched Mrs Mitchell make sandwiches instead.

They went down the back steps carrying plates of food close to their bodies. Tiny sandwiches, thick sausage rolls, bits of hard cheese poked on toothpicks and decorated with slices of salami. The others stood back to make a path to the table. Susie looked around. She knew Lisa and most of her friends. Maria and Anita from year eight wore spiked heels and tight skirts. They stood taller than any of the boys. Michelle's brother Mark was there and a couple of boys with their backs to the girls.

Susie took a drink and stood close to Sonya. She looked around the yard. Two thick bushes in pots blocked the side lane. Hard to leave that way. Beyond the clothesline was a lemon tree, an old tool shed and then the paling fence. It was too dark to make out if there was still a back gate or not. In the far corner were thick oleander and hibiscus bushes and a frangipani tree.

Six years old. Kim, Susie, Sonya and Michelle play hide-and-seek in Sonya's backyard. Susie and Kim hide behind the red hibiscus, bury their faces in the trumpet flowers. They breathe the rich smell in, are discovered and run back home to the clothesline, the yellow pollen fresh on their lips.

It was hot.

Susie took a sausage roll and stepped back from the table. The bandaid under her arm itched. She held her cold glass to her forehead and it left a wet mark on her skin. Sweat ran down the backs of her knees. Hands grabbed at plates of food. Suddenly there were more people than before. Someone knocked over a glass of juice.

'Watch out.'

'Watch what you're doing.'

'Hey, Tom, get us a drink, will you?'

*Tom.*

He was tall, lanky, with curly black hair. He had three sausage rolls piled one on top of the other and two glasses of juice. She tried to see his face but he was side-on to her and all she could make out was the silhouette of a large nose, glowing in the red and orange light. She turned away.

*What happened to noses when you kissed? To that nose? Did it go left or right? What if you went the wrong way?* She drummed her black fingernails on the glass.

Tanya was standing close to Nick and he was playing with a piece of her hair. Lisa had moved the tape recorder to the top of the back steps and was dancing on the grass. She beckoned Maria and Anita to join in.

*Maybe it wouldn't be too bad. Maybe he'd just go peck like one of Mum's friends at Christmas. Maybe he wouldn't want to do anything. But what if he was like on television . . . lips pressing hard . . . head forced back . . . tongue . . . ?*

Susie moved closer to Michelle and Cheryl. Michelle's brother's friend was there too.

'. . . this really beaut party. Mum and Dad went out and we . . .'

*But if he didn't want to do anything, that meant she was a dag. Or at least he thought she was.*

She watched him from the corner of her eye. He had passed one of the drinks to Nick but he was eating all the sausage rolls at once. Great, gaping mouth. Long arms waving as he spoke.

*What about those long arms . . . ? Will he try to wrap them around . . . Bend at the knees . . . Move forward . . . In the dark . . . The others waiting, counting . . . Big nose to the left or the right . . . Sloppy wet lips . . . The smell of tomato sauce . . . In the dark behind the clotheslines, the lemon tree, the tool shed.*

'C'mon, Susie.' Sonya slipped her arm through hers. 'Mum and Dad have gone to bed. Lisa says it's time to play.'

# Chapter 13

'O.K., everyone.' Lisa stood on the bottom step and clapped her hands.

Anita turned the music right down and stood beside her.

*Like teachers on assembly.*

'You all get a piece of paper with a number on it. When I call the numbers you have to find your partner and go down the back . . .' Lisa rolled her eyes, waved a hand towards the dark space behind the lemon tree and swivelled her hips.

'What do we have to do?'

'Yeah, Lisa, give us a demo.'

Lisa laughed and put one hand on her hip. 'If you don't know . . .' she said. Then she threw her head back like someone in a movie and jumped down. Maria passed her a small cardboard box and she moved around the yard, handing out small hard balls of screwed-up paper.

'Like your hair,' she said to Susie. 'But no one wears *green* eyeshadow.' She moved towards Nick and Tanya.

Susie unravelled the paper.

*Not number one. Thank God.*

She looked around the yard.

'O.K. O.K. O.K.' Lisa clapped her hands again. 'Who's got number one?'

Tanya and Nick waved their hands.

'Rigged. Y' rigged it.'

'Go on,' called Lisa. 'We've all got to count.'

Nick put his arm across Tanya's shoulders and pulled her close to him.

'No one's allowed to look,' he said as they headed for the darkness.

Tanya was giggling and looking up at him.

Susie turned away. Michelle's brother started a slow handclap.

'One, two, three, four . . .' The boys squatted on the ground and called the numbers. Susie's hands were sweating. She unrolled the piece of paper again. Number two. *Next!*

'. . . nine, ten, eleven, twelve . . .'

*Next! In the darkness with the counting. Those arms.*

She spun round quickly. Anita and Maria were standing in front of the side lane. Lisa guarded the steps to the house.

*Race over. Say I have to go to the toilet. I'm going to be sick.*

Susie rubbed her damp hands down the legs of her jeans. Sweat ran down the back of her neck.

'. . . eighteen, nineteen, twenty . . .'

'Hurry up, you two.'

'Give someone else a turn.'

'. . . twenty-seven, twenty-eight, twenty-nine . . .'

*Stay all night. I'm next.*

Sonya had moved onto the grass with Michelle and Cheryl. She leant forward and called Susie to come and sit with them.

'What number are you?'

'Next.' Susie didn't take her eyes off the dark place at the end of the yard.

'. . . thirty-five, thirty-six, thirty-seven . . .'

*I am not going to do it. Stupid game. When we get there, I'll just tell him. I'll say, Listen, I don't kiss anyone just because Lisa Mitchell says so. Nothing personal.*

'. . . forty-four, forty-five, forty-six . . .'

The lower branches of the lemon tree were pushed aside and Nick and Tanya came back into the light. There were claps and cheers.

Susie looked for Tom.

Tanya grinned up at Nick and then down at her friends on the grass.

'Number two. Who's number two?' Lisa was leaping around on the step again.

Susie sat frozen.

*Jump up. Say you're not going to do it. Say you have to go home right now. They'll laugh. They'll say . . .*

'Me!' shouted Tom. He danced into the space in front of Lisa. 'Who's the lucky girl?'

'It's Susie. It's Susie,' yelled Sonya.

*Some friend.*

'And she's going to chicken out . . .'

'I am not.' Susie stood up and faced Tom. 'It's me. Let's go.'

She led the way down the path to the tree. He caught up with her in a few strides and put his arm across her shoulder the way Nick had done with Tanya. His arm was hot and heavy and it bounced awkwardly because he was so tall and his long legs had trouble slowing down for hers.

'One, two, three . . .'

Past the lemon tree, the hibiscus, the tool shed. They stopped under the frangipani.

'. . . seven, eight, nine . . .'

Susie didn't look at him. She studied the thick stubby branches, then reached out to scratch at the grey trunk.

101

At her feet there were flowers, their edges curled and brown.

'My name's Tom.'

'I know.'

He reached up and held onto a branch. He swung forward for a moment, testing his weight. The branch scraped against the fence.

'. . . fifteen, sixteen, seventeen . . .'

'We don't have to do anything if you don't want to,' he said. 'We can just go back and say we did, if you like.'

*Dag. Ugly. Say you want to kiss me, to hold my hand here in the dark, not just when the others were looking.*

'. . . twenty-three, twenty-four, twenty-five . . .'

'When we go back we'll just grin and not say anything when they ask.' Tom raised his eyebrows and looked at her, waiting for her to nod. 'Or if you like . . .' He reached out a hand and touched her shoulder. His hand was hot and sweaty. He closed his eyes and his face moved towards hers.

'No,' she said. 'I think this is a really daggy party.' She stepped back.

*Be like Tanya. Giggle. Smile sweetly.* She glanced at him quickly and looked away again.

'I'm sick of this game and I'm sick of this place. I'm getting out of here.'

She held on to the lowest branch of the tree with one hand and pulled herself up onto the fence.

'. . . thirty, thirty-one, thirty-two . . .'

'Hang on. You can't. What'll I tell the others?' His hands hung loosely at his sides.

'Tell 'em what you like.' She started to climb down into the lane. 'Tell Lisa that you kissed me so hard that I flew off into orbit.'

'I'll come with you.' He pulled himself up onto the

fence. 'You might get bashed up on the way home.'

'No way. What good would you be?'

'. . . forty-four, forty-five, forty-six . . .'

'Come on you two, give someone else a go!'

Susie let go. She looked up the long, dark lane and then back through the gap in the fence. Tom was standing, staring at his feet, his shoulders hunched. She could still call him, have some company up past the station, the pub, home. She turned away.

'. . . fifty-one, fifty-two, fifty-three . . .'

She started to run. Bright pink and green neon flashed where the lane joined King Street. There would be people there, going in and out of pubs, restaurants. Lots of people. She glanced quickly over her shoulder. Nothing moved in the shadows. It was hot, stifling, the sticky heat that comes before rain. An overhanging branch brushed against her face. The bright lights came closer. A tomcat squealed and leapt off the high galvanised iron fence.

She came out onto King Street between the St Vincent de Paul shop and the Burmese restaurant. Trucks slowed at the lights and she breathed in the exhaust fumes. A crowd hung round the entrance to the railway station. Dogs barked.

'C'mon, you've had·enough. Let's go . . .'

'No. Give it to me . . .'

Susie pushed through the crowd and stopped at the crossing.

'You're a nicegirl.' The old man beside her said it as one word.

'Anicegirl,' he repeated.

The light changed and she crossed quickly. The red light came back on as she reached the far footpath and she looked around to see the old man still in the middle of the road. Car horns blared.

She went on slowly. The doors to the coffee shops were open and people inside were laughing and drinking. Piano music came from one. She stopped and looked in the window of the bookshop. She smelt curry, pizza sauce, the hot summer night. She trailed her hand along the window of the shop as she walked.

Outside the newsagent's was a boy not much bigger than herself. He turned around and she recognised him as one who lived up the road from Kim's and used to play cricket with them, last summer. He looked up as Susie passed him and then followed her.

'Hey,' he called. 'Hey, do you want to go somewhere?'

She walked more quickly.

'I'm talking to you, slag.'

She looked down and hurried. Past the fish shop and the butcher. Past a couple looking in the window of the furniture shop. Susie glanced back. He wasn't following her. Sweat ran down her face and the backs of her legs.

*Cold showers. Icecreams. A swim.*

A long way away was the sound of thunder.

Ahead was the pub. Men stood in the doorway. They spread over the footpath and squatted in the gutter. They sat on the hoods of the cars and on the back of the vegetable shop truck. The sound of the trots at Harold Park blared from a car radio.

' 'night, luv.'

'Where're you off to, sweetheart?'

'Stand aside, let her through.'

They stood back, watching her, flicking their cigarette ash away from her.

Someone whistled, long and low.

She was round the corner. Three blocks to go. Past

the playground and the shop. She counted her steps. *One, two, three . . .*

'Susie.'

She turned. Someone was following her. Someone tall, his long arms dangling.

*Tom.*

She waited till he got a bit closer.

'Well?' she said and couldn't look directly at him.

'I just thought I'd follow you.' He put his hands in his pockets and leaned against the telephone pole.

'Look, I'm all right. I can look after myself.'

They stood there for a moment, saying nothing. A light wind whipped the papers in the gutter.

' 's going to rain,' said Tom. 'D'you want to go back up to King Street and get a drink?'

Susie hesitated.

*High school kids sit around drinking and sharing cakes. Their legs brush under the table.*

She felt a raindrop in her hair. Then another. She looked down.

'No,' she said. 'I think I'd better go home. You should go back to the party. I'll see you.'

She turned and started to run. This time she didn't look back but bent her head into the rain and the wind. Lightning lit up the sky. More thunder. She ducked to miss a low branch and banged her ankle against something lying on the footpath. A siren wailed from the direction of the hospital. More rain. Thunder. Lightning, as she leapt across the gutter and raced down the next block. Home. She kicked the gate open and ran round the side of the house. Rain pelted down against the walls. It poured from the hole in the guttering above the kitchen. It soaked through her clothes and plastered them to her body.

Susie pushed at the laundry window. It was always

unlocked. It was just big enough for her to climb through.

The window didn't give. She pushed again. Her key was upstairs in her tunic pocket. *Damn you, Mum. Why tonight?* She tried to lever the window open. She rattled it. She punched at the wall below it and then slumped back against the bricks. All the other windows were barred. She ran to the kitchen and pressed her face to the metal. The plates from dinner were still in the sink. The light had been left on and it shone warmly on the wooden table.

'Mum,' shouted Susie and shook the bars.

Her voice was lost in the drumming of rain on the bricks and the tin roof.

'Mum!'

# Chapter 14

Susie pressed herself flat against the wall.

*Stay here? Run? Next door? Back to the party? Somewhere? Anywhere?*

Her eyes closed and her head dropped forward. A blast of wind and rain shook her awake. She ran back up the path and out onto the darkened street.

*Run. Get dry. Sleep.*

She hunched her shoulders and ran past the Watsons' and McGregors', past the playground and through the lanes. Rain stung her face. Her wet clothes were heavy.

*Sonya, all the kids warm on the floor. Giggling, laughing. Can't go back.*

She drew her jacket tightly across her chest. She stopped at the Australia Street corner and leant against the lamppost, puffing. Cars raced past. She ducked back behind a fence. *Don't see me.* Without thinking she ran across the road, towards the cemetery and the church.

The wind bowled her along. It picked up the tops of the trees and tossed them against the black sky. It sent shadows hurtling over the grass.

*Don't ever come home across the park at night.*

*You don't know how some people can be.*

*This town is full of crazy people. Weirdos.*

All round the edges of the park shone the warm dry

squares of light in people's houses. Strangers sitting talking, curled up in bed, watching television, listening to music and to the rain.

*Run to them. Beat on the doors. Let me in. Let me in.*

She fell, picked herself up, staggered against the sandstone wall, coughing and gasping.

The chains on the swing rattled. Susie spun round.

*If someone was there? Waiting. Watching from the trees? The bushes? The wall?*

*Waiting to grab . . .*

Thud. Thud. The end of the seesaw bounced with each gust of wind.

Thud. Thud.

She screamed. Her voice was lost in the noise of the wind. She ran down the smooth bike track, past the place where the kids played cricket.

*I'm talking to you, slag.*

Past the place where the bonfires and crackers were every year. The bamboo behind the wall creaked and groaned.

*Run.*

Susie got to the end of the path. She raced round the corner, charged into someone, bowled them over, screamed and rolled with them into the gutter.

'My God, it's you!' The Blue Lady stood up. She grabbed for her umbrella and held out a hand to Susie. 'Are you all right?' Susie sat still as the water surged around her.

'C'mon,' said the woman. 'You can't stay there. Though heaven only knows what you're doing racing round in the dead of night.' She struggled as the wind blew her umbrella inside out. 'Does your mother know where you are?'

Susie didn't answer. She stood up. Her head ached and she had cracked her knee on the cement.

'Quick,' the Blue Lady said and pushed Susie across the road to her gate. She opened it and went up the steps to the door.

'Come on,' she opened the door and switched on the light. Still Susie didn't move.

'You can't stay out in this weather. You'll get a chill or whatever it is that wet clothes do to a person.' The Blue Lady left the open door and came back down the steps to the footpath. The light from the hallway shone on her wet hair though her face was still in darkness.

'I am not going to eat you. You cannot stay out in this rain.' She paused for a minute and drew back slightly. 'Are you afraid of me?'

'You're crazy,' whispered Susie. 'Everyone says so. Kim and . . . And Mrs Watson told my Mum.'

'Mrs Watson? Betty Watson?' The Blue Lady stood with one hand on the gate, the wind blowing the loose strands of hair across her face. 'Just what exactly did Mrs Watson say?'

Susie looked down.

'You can tell me . . .' The woman's voice was soft. 'I think I already know.'

'She said . . . She said you got jilted and went crazy and ran away and then you came back and you don't talk to anyone that you used to know.'

Susie kept her eyes on the woman's yellow-stained hands. The Blue Lady turned and went back to the verandah. She closed the door, picked up the umbrella and came back down the steps. 'Betty Watson is a stupid old woman,' she said. She stood close to Susie and jabbed her chest with one finger. 'I want to show you something.' She looked across at the cemetery and then back at Susie. 'You're not scared of the graveyard at night, are you?'

109

Susie blinked. *Go there. With her. Now.* She shook her head.

'Come on, then.' The woman grabbed Susie's hand. From a pocket in her skirt, she took a small flashlight.

Susie looked at the wild blowing shadows of the park and the cemetery. The rain still poured down the back of her neck. The thick material of her jeans rubbed the inside of her legs as she crossed the road. The woman looked straight ahead as they followed the tiny point of light down the gravel path, past the church door, past the gap in the trees that led through to the grave of the boy who was lost at sea. Susie ran to keep up. She started to ask, 'Where are we . . .' but her voice was picked up and lost in the wind. They veered slightly to the left and went under the Chinese elms and then stopped before a clump of trees that had branches sweeping down to the ground.

'Do you know who's buried there?' the woman was shouting over the wind and rain.

*Snails. Slide and squash on the floor.*

*Can you tell us where we can find the grave of Eliza Donnithorne?*

'Eliza Donnithorne. That's who. Does that mean anything to you?'

Susie shook her head. The woman lifted a branch aside and they stepped closer to the stone. With the tip of her umbrella she pointed to the inscription:

AND OF HIS DAUGHTER, ELIZA EMILY DONNITHORNE. DIED 20TH MAY 1866.

'There,' she said, 'was a mad woman. She *was* jilted on her wedding day and stayed in her wedding dress till the day she died. She kept the door on the latch and the table

110

laid, just in case he ever changed his mind and came back to her. Thirty years she waited – or so they reckon. There's a book and a film about her. That's madness.' Her voice was hoarse from shouting. She brushed the wild strands of hair from around her face. 'There's another sort of madness. Marrying someone you don't love just because you've been stupid enough to get engaged because all your friends were doing it and you believed what you'd always been taught – that you're only half a person on your own, that you need someone else to make you complete.'

Rain dripped from her hair.

'I grew up in that house.' She waved the umbrella back towards the gate. 'I played over here when I was a kid, just like you and your friend. I knew the story of this woman and I'd just laughed at it. But just before I was to get married, a couple of days before, I was over here and I saw this grave again and I had a good think about it.' She sat down on the flat stone, her voice so soft now that Susie had to sit beside her to hear what she was saying.

'I thought about a woman so taken up with another person – so scared of facing life alone, without him, that she'd waste thirty years, shutting out the world, rather than face his betrayal. She narrowed her life down to one tiny part, and lived in that.

'I also thought about being married and what it meant to women like me. In a few years I'd be stuck with a tribe of kids, worried only about getting dinner on time, and I'd never do the things *I* wanted to do. The night before the wedding I cleared out. I went to see him but he was out with his mates getting drunk so I wrote him a note. I didn't care what everyone thought. It was between him and me and I knew it wouldn't work. I also knew that unlike Eliza here there was no way that I'd sit around because I didn't have a man. I had a whole host of things

111

I wanted to do.' She paused. 'And I've done them too.'

She stood up slowly, and they pushed their way through the branches and started to walk back along the path. 'Correction. I'm still doing them,' she said. 'You can tell your Mrs Smarty-pants Watson that Jess Fisher doesn't speak to her on the street because I've got nothing to say to her. She always was an old gossip.'

The wind and the rain had eased. The Blue Lady didn't bother to put the umbrella up but walked slowly, her face held up to the drizzle.

When they got to the big tree by the gate she turned to Susie and said, 'I don't know why I'm telling you all this.' Susie didn't reply.

'You'd better come over home and get dry. We'll ring your mother then. And, eh, by the way, you know I'm Jess. You're Sue, aren't you?'

'Susannah.' She'd never said it to anyone like that before. That's how it was written on report cards, what new teachers said.

'How do you do, Susannah. I'm pleased to meet you at last.' Jess bent her head slightly as if they were being formally introduced. You couldn't be sure what expression her face was wearing in the shadow.

Susie took her wet clothes off in the bathroom and rubbed herself dry with a thick towel. She pulled the bandaid off from under her arm and flushed it down the toilet. Then she put on an old-fashioned man's dressing gown with big cuffs and wide, purple lapels. There were no mirrors in the room so she ran her fingers through her wet hair. It still stood out in short spikes.

When she went through to the kitchen, Jess wasn't there. Susie picked up one of the steaming cups of coffee from the table and moved slowly around the room. The wallpaper was the same bright yellow sunflowers with shiny green leaves. She touched the spot above the stove where two sheets joined and the edges curled. The calendar from the garage on King Street was gone. So were the bills and the notes from school stuck on the fridge with tiny magnets. But there were drawings, dozens of them, on sheets of paper, some as small as a pocket notebook, taped on the walls, the window frame and the cupboard door. Her eyes went from sketches of birds, some flying, some perched on twigs, to insects, lizards, leaves and pods, formations of rock and stone, tree trunks, roots and their branches. She picked up a wooden frame from the mantelpiece. Three photographs were set into an inner sheet of cardboard. One was a snapshot of a baby, a fat child sprawled naked on a rug on a lawn. The next was a toddler with thick dark curly hair and brown eyes. Her arms were outstretched, reaching up to the photographer. In the final photo, a girl about Susie's age was sitting on a couch, looking up from a book, with a woman about Susie's mother's age. The girl had long black plaits falling over her shoulders. The dress she was wearing was tinted blue. It had short puffed sleeves and a rounded white collar. There was something familiar about the woman. Her shoulder-length hair was dark brown and wavy.

Susie moved into the middle of the kitchen, and held the photograph under the light. The woman was Jess, a much younger Jess, but her dress was red. In the bottom corner of the cardboard frame was stamped the word, 'Paris'.

*Was that where she went? Was this the daughter? Where is she now?*

Susie heard footsteps in the hall. She put the photos back, not quite in the same place as before, and sat down as Jess came into the room.

113

Jess glanced at the mantelpiece and looked back at Susie, but said nothing.

Susie waved her hand at the sketches pinned around the room.

'You must be always drawing,' she said, quickly.

Jess shrugged. 'You'd better ring your mum, don't you think?'

Susie counted fifteen rings before she hung up. She came back in from the hall and sat down in the kitchen. 'She's not answering,' she said.

Jess frowned.

'It's all right,' said Susie. 'She went to a party.' She looked down. 'I'm supposed to be at Sonya's place.' She twisted the mug in her hands. 'But there was this game and I didn't want to play and I cleared out and I'm supposed to be sleeping there 'cause Mum's coming home really late but it doesn't matter because Sonya's mum thinks my mum picked me up . . .' She slumped forward onto her elbow on the table. She was suddenly tired again and hungry.

'Well,' said the Blue Lady, holding her coffee cup in the air and raising an eyebrow, 'you'd better stay here then.' She smiled at Susie then, for the first time, and chuckled. 'Here's to running away.'

They sat and ate a plate of toast dripping with cheese, and half a packet of chocolate biscuits.

*Ask about the drawings. Ask about the girl in the photo. Ask . . .*

'I suppose you used to come in here often when your friend lived here,' said Jess.

Susie nodded. 'I used to stay the night and if we couldn't sleep we'd come down here and eat and watch a video.'

114

'You were good friends, then,' said Jess.

'She's only sent me one lousy postcard.'

The woman didn't answer. She stood up and cleared the table. 'It's after midnight, Susannah,' she said. 'I think we should get some sleep. Do you want to curl up on the couch?'

Susie took a deep breath. 'Can I, umm . . . When I used to come I slept in Kim's room.'

'Oh? And which room was that?'

'Upstairs. At the front.'

The woman turned away and put the cups in the sink.

'Is that where you sleep?' said Susie.

'No. It's my workroom. You can sleep there.'

Susie followed Jess from the room. As she closed the door, she looked back at the photos on the mantelpiece. The eyes of the girl seemed to be looking straight at her.

'You watched me dyeing, didn't you?' the Blue Lady said.

Susie nodded.

*Don't ask me why I ran. I don't know.*

'Well, now you'll see what I do with all that wool.'

'It's our tree.' Susie stood in the doorway and stared at the far wall. The beds and the wardrobes were gone. So too were the posters, the whole wall papered with Uncanny X-men, Hoodoo Gurus, Kids in the Kitchen. Instead, there was a huge wooden frame. Strings ran from almost on the floor to the top crosspiece and there were other bits of wood cutting across the strings above an unfinished tapestry. Baskets of wool covered the floor.

'I'm still working on this,' said the woman. She stood in front of the work and indicated two finished tapestries hanging on the wall on either side of her. 'It's a panel to go with those two. When I'm finished I'll stitch the three together. Stand over here and imagine them all joined.'

115

She touched Susie on the arm and they moved into the centre of the room.

'It's our tree,' said Susie again. She ran to the window and looked across at the huge Moreton Bay fig, near the cemetery gate. She looked back at the tapestry. The central panel, the one still on the loom, was the twisting, thrusting upheaval of roots from the soil. Then there was the trunk, solid, broad, and the branches, moving out in all directions, covered with shiny green summer leaves.

Susie stepped back and half-closed one eye so the edges of the panel on the loom melted into the edges of the completed panels that hung on the walls.

'It's more than that,' said Jess, softly.

'Can I touch it?'

Jess nodded.

Susie knelt and reached out to feel the thick woven texture. She ran her hands over the birds and insects, made to stand out on the ground at the foot of the tree. She felt other things. Real bits of grass, bark and stone were woven into the fabric. Real pods spilled their seed on the ground. She tried to take in the whole work: on her left the church reduced to a square beneath the spreading branches, the steeple drawn on it the way she drew in kindergarten. On her right were the gravestones, sandy-coloured rectangles, lying scattered, covered by long grass, by more birds and by two playing children.

'That's us,' said Susie.

'Could be,' said the woman.

Susie leant back and looked to the top of the finished panels. The branches reached up and out, the leaves filled the space above her. Some of the leaves were young and fresh, woven in pale green. As she looked down the work, the colour changed and grew darker, older. The fruit too began firm and green but further down was fuller, more brown and around the base of the tree was fallen and split, shedding seeds on the ground. Some lay there, barely discernible from the soil while others were being pecked at by the birds.

'It's . . .' Susie stood up. She tried to find the word to say what the tapestry made her feel. She blinked to hold back tears.

'It's . . . I never thought you did stuff like this. I thought . . .'

*Witch. Crazy.*

She put her head down and reached out to touch the figures.

The woman took some of the tan-coloured wool from a basket. 'This colour is made from all the lichen I've been scraping off the headstones. Watch.' She gathered some of the vertical threads of the unfinished panel and held them forward. She slipped the wool in her hand behind them, leaving a long piece dangling at the back. Forwards and back she went, firming down each row, building up a thin strip.

'It's all part of a branch,' she said. 'There are leaves to go in all round it. Pass me some of the dark green.' Susie passed the wool and then stepped back. She put her head on one side. She tried to look at the tapestry, to take it all in at once, but her eyes kept stopping on little things. The way a black and white magpie was swooping on a coloured stone, the hint of yellow on the underside of a leaf, the kid's hair that streamed back as she ran.

*Weirdo. Witch. Crazy.*

'Why is the tree bigger than the church?' she said at last.

The woman shrugged. 'That's the way I see it in my head.'

Susie sat on the floor and leant back against the only heavy chair in the room. It faced the window. She could hear the rain still hitting the iron roof over the balcony.

'I sit in it,' the woman said, 'when I don't know what to do next and I just want to think.'

She watched the woman's hands working, the fingers lifting the fine vertical threads and weaving the small patches of colour, building up the total picture.

On either side of the pieces hanging on the wall were more sketches like the ones in the kitchen. There were others too, sketches of children at play. Figures were jumping and running, climbing and swinging from trees and solid blocks of stone. Susie and Kim.

'Did you draw us so you could put us in it?' Susie asked.

There was silence for a moment. The rain stopped and there was only the sound of dripping from a leak in the balcony roof. Beside the loom and the long wallhangings, Jess looked suddenly small and tired.

'Sort of . . . but I used to play there too. That was a heck of a long time ago and I think you reminded me of myself.'

Susie curled up in the chair under a rug. Jess turned out the light.

'Goodnight, Susannah. If you need me, I'm just in the next room,' she said.

Susie sat in the dark for a long time. As her eyes got used to it, she saw again the huge shape of the loom, the sweeping twisted shadows of the tree.

*Where exactly did she play . . . ? On the stone of Eliza Donnithorne . . . ? Did she have a friend who she went there with . . . ? Did she know about the secret postbox then . . . ? Why weave the tree . . . ? What will she do with it when it's finished . . . ? Why give me the drawings . . . ? Where did she go when she ran away . . . ? Was that girl the same as the baby . . . ? Her daughter . . . ? Why did she come*

118

*back . . . ? Why does she always wear blue . . . ? How much more is there to know about her . . . ?*

*Like the tapestry . . . each time you look there's more to know . . . how much more have I missed . . . Is everyone so complicated . . . ?*

# Chapter 15

Susie woke up in the big chair, a light blanket across her knees. Sunlight streamed in the open doors that led to the balcony. Beyond it she could see only the tree, its broad branches stretching out over the footpath, filling the sky. She turned to the tapestry and found herself grinning at the warm colours, the richness of line and familiar detail.

'Susannah!'

She smelt coffee and toast, heard doors opening and a tap running. She got up and dressed quickly and went downstairs.

'I'll have to go home,' Susie said. 'Mum'll have a fit if Mrs Mitchell rings. I'd better tell her first.'

'I'll ring her if you want me to.'

Susie shook her head. 'I'd rather tell her myself.'

'As you like.' Jess passed her a piece of toast. 'It's going to be a lovely day today. Hard to believe after last night.'

Susie sipped her coffee, hesitated for a minute and then looked at the woman. 'Can I come again and watch? I won't get in the way or anything. I could pass you the wool or hang it out for you when you're dyeing.'

Jess spread her toast with orange marmalade. 'I was going to ask if you'd like to, but you didn't give me time.'

Susie crossed the park in the sunshine. She had her jacket slung over her shoulder and she leapt over the cracks in the cement as if the holidays had already begun. Across the rooftops she could see clear to the mountains. She didn't look back at the swings or the seesaw.

When she got home, she went down the side path to the kitchen door. It was open and her mother stood at the sink, filling the kettle.

'Hi, there,' she said and leant over to give Susie a kiss on the forehead. 'I didn't think you lot would be up for hours. How was the party?'

'O.K.' said Susie. 'How was yours?'

'Great.'

They sat across the table from each other. Susie's mother leant on her elbows and looked at her daughter. 'I saw all these people that I haven't seen for ages and ages. Great food. He had a roast sucking pig. Can you believe that? We all stuffed ourselves. Then we just danced and danced. I didn't get home till about three.' She got up and put some bread in the toaster. 'Did they like your hair?'

Susie sat back in her chair.

'Mum,' she said, without looking up, 'I cleared out from the party.'

'You what?' Her mother stepped back towards the table.

'Don't go off your brain or anything. I'm O.K. I just want to tell you what I did.'

'Where have you been? Where did you sleep?'

'I'm trying to tell you.' She paused. Her clenched fists rested on the table.

Her mother sat down, slowly.

Susie finished.

Her mother stopped fiddling with the knife and the crumbs of toast on the white plate. 'Oh, Suse.' She got up and put her arms around her daughter and kissed her hair as she used to do when Susie was little. 'I wish I'd known how you were feeling.' She held her that way, tightly, for a long time.

They swam in the afternoon. Susie practised dropping a twenty cent piece on the bottom of the pool and duck-diving to get it. When she got out she shook herself dry, showering her mother with fine drops of water. She rolled over, gasping.

They lay in the sun eating slices of cool rockmelon.

'Mum?'

'Mmm.'

'Remember you said once I'd want to know more about my father . . .'

'Mmm.'

'Well . . . Do you think I'll ever get to meet him?' *Tell me.*

Her mother rolled over and leant up on her elbow. 'He's coming back to Australia to live,' she said slowly. 'In a few months. I had a letter from him. He wants to know you.'

Susie sat up and hugged her knees. 'But if he didn't want me before, how come he wants me now?'

'I don't know. I don't know what he's thinking or how he's changed. I don't know anything.'

'But what'll I say to him?'

Her mother shrugged. 'I don't know. I don't even know what *I'll* say to him. But that doesn't matter. I'll be with you when you see him.'

'Are you two going to get married again?'

Her mother sat up and laughed. 'No way, Suse. That sort of thing only happens in bad movies.' She patted her daughter's knee. 'It'll be a bit hard at first but you might find out that he's really nice and you like him.'

'Do you want to see him, Mum?'

Her mother stood up. 'To be honest, I don't know. Don't get too many romantic ideas about us, Suse. If he'd come back years ago, things might have been different, but we've all changed. You and I have got a pretty good life and I'm not going to let in anything that's going to hurt that.' She picked up her towel and shook the grass from it. 'I'm glad you asked about him. I've been waiting for the right moment to tell you.'

Michelle rang. 'You should have seen the look on Lisa's face when you two didn't come back. What happened? What did you do? What's he like?'

She invited Susie to sleep at her place on the first weekend of the holidays and Susie said, 'Yes'.

Tom rang. Susie was at the shop. Her mother told her the minute she walked in.

'What did he want?' she said and avoided her mother's eyes.

'I don't know. I told him to ring back in ten minutes.'

Susie put the milk away and sat on the step that led from the dining room into the kitchen and jumped at every tiny sound until he did.

And Susie went upstairs and moved things. She put the bed under the window and the desk in the centre of the room. She climbed on them and took down the kite, the posters, the drawings and the photographs. She stuffed all the things into the wardrobe, stood and looked at the bare walls and felt good. She had nothing new to put up, yet. She would paint her room when the holidays began. The project book still lay on the desk. She flicked through it, adding a bit more colour to the drawing of the city, more detail to the borders of each page. Her eyes rested on the incomplete section, the whited-out spaces.

She leant over and wrote.

> *I will be an artist.*
> *I will run the circus.*
> *I will be the ringmaster . . .*

Kim will not come for Christmas, but she will write for Susie's birthday. Susie won't write back straight away.

Susie will not speak to David until they are put together to work in the same science group in high school.

And Susie will go back and back to see Jess. She will pass her the wool until it is finished and then she will help cut the tapestry from the loom and they will sit cross-legged on the floor and stitch together the pieces of their tree.

Susie's mother will take her to the hairdresser's. Susie will say, 'Come on, Mum. You too.' And her mother will, at first, shake her head but then they will both sit with bright shiny cloths around their shoulders. And Susie's spikes will be evened and straightened and her mother's old stretched curls will fall to the floor. They will leave, laughing at the reflection they see in the mirror outside the butcher's shop window. Her mother will wait till the noise of the trucks on King Street dies a little and she will clutch the wisps of hair around her ears and say, 'Oh, Suse, how could I do this?'

And her daughter will turn her back on the reflections in the glass and standing almost as tall as her mother, will say, 'I'm not Suse, I am Susannah.'